NUGLY

Also by M. C. Ross

A Dog's Porpoise

Game Over

NUGLY

M. C. ROSS

SCHOLASTIC INC.

ISBN 978-1-338-82718-7

10 9 8 7 6 5 4 3 2 1   23 24 25 26 27

Printed in the U.S.A.   40
First printing 2023

Book design by Maithili Joshi

DEDICATED TO PAT, SARA, AND GORDY, ALL OF WHOM HELPED THIS BOOK GET FINISHED. SOME MORE HELPFULLY THAN OTHERS. (LOOKING AT YOU, GORDON.)

Part One

NUGGET

1

The Number One Main Thing

The number one main thing a dog does every day is: fall in love. Dogs do this over and over again, often without really thinking about it, the same way you and I sneeze or blink at bright lights.

The second main thing a dog does is: be hungry. That one's pretty self-explanatory.

Within five seconds of Nugget being born, he did both.

Being born is a bit overwhelming, so it was sort of nice that Nugget had something to focus on. Also playing in his favor was the fact that puppies are unable to open their eyes for ten to fourteen days after they're born. This is a very smart system. Imagine going from never having seen anything at all to seeing a crowded room with lots of people all paying attention to you. It'd be a lot to take in. You'd want some time to adjust. Like, say, one to two weeks. This is exactly the amount of time puppies get, and just one of the many ways in which humans have yet to catch up to dogs.

But even though he couldn't see that he'd been born,

Nugget could certainly feel it—and smell it. One moment his entire universe had been warm and extremely compact. Now there was air on his fur, and that warmth, which had previously been all around him, was suddenly behind him, big and soft and breathing in and out. To Nugget's nose—which even from birth could smell things no human would ever be able to—the big warm thing smelled like comfort and courage and *home*. And a voice, delighted, came from on high: "Aw, look at that cute little nugget!"

Nugget had been born and named in a single instant. Again, a bit overwhelming. But just before Nugget could panic, that big, warm, good-smelling presence beside him stood up, shifted around, and plopped back down right in front of him, where it proceeded to lick his face urgently. *Hello*, those licks said. *Don't worry. I'm here for you. You're safe. It's okay.*

That's when Nugget realized: This was his mother.

That was also the first time Nugget loved someone.

He'd get a chance to try it out again soon. Like, right now. Because, all of a sudden, his mom was standing back up and turning away from Nugget. His tiny heart, just a few *ba-bumps* into its professional career, nearly stopped. Why had she left him? Was this forever? But no—within moments Nugget's mother had completed a full rotation, and when she returned, she used her nose to nudge someone right up next to Nugget. Someone just as small as Nugget, and just as wriggly, and just as eager to get a big, wet, sloppy face bath from their mother.

Nugget's heartbeat came back twice as fast. A sibling. He had a sibling!

Soon came another puppy, and another, and pretty soon Nugget had six brothers and sisters, and he loved each one of them more than the last. Or, wait, no—he loved each one of them just as much as the last. Or, hold on, wait—well, actually, Nugget wasn't too worried about the details just yet. Love, in Nugget's case, was quite literally blind.

And, anyway, he had more pressing things to focus on right now. Because while all this had been happening—while he and his siblings had been entering the world, and while the voices from on high had been cooing and conversing amongst themselves, and while his mother had been making sure each and every puppy received a warm welcome—Nugget had also been experiencing another feeling for the first time ever. It was a constant dull ache, like waves on a beach, and it pushed him and his siblings toward their mother.

Because Nugget was a dog, and therefore, Nugget was hungry.

Again: pretty self-explanatory.

As he enjoyed his mother's milk for the first time, squeezed up between his siblings almost as tightly as they had been before they were born, Nugget decided that on the whole, being alive seemed like a pretty good state of affairs.

But if that tiny heartbeat ever fluttered in those first few minutes—if doubt ever flickered behind Nugget's closed eyes—it was because some part of him still remembered those terrible seconds when his mother had turned away from him. When, for a second, Nugget held out all the love he had to give in his little body and felt the terrible fear of not knowing if that love would be returned.

Later, when people spoke about Nugget, they would say he was different from other dogs. Unique. Some would mean it in a nice way; others would not. Almost all of them would be referring to the parts of Nugget that were easiest to notice, that even a stranger could see.

But from his very first breath, Nugget had been unique in a much less obvious way. What set him apart was this: He had so much love in him that he could change people's lives. It was so much love that it felt like it might give him unimaginable strength—or tear him apart.

In time, it would do both.

For now, Nugget just enjoyed the feeling of being safe and happy and taken care of and loved by his family with no questions or hesitations. It took precedence over any other worries he may have had.

It was the number one main thing.

2
Nugget's Family

Nugget had a mother, three brothers, and three sisters. That first night, all of Nugget's siblings got their names in more or less the same fashion as Nugget, which was how he wound up with three brothers named Biscuit, Bacon, and Frosty, and three sisters named Pepper, Sprite, and Cheese Fries. As far as Nugget was concerned, his mother's name was Mom, but according to those voices he'd heard earlier, she could also be referred to as Wendy, so that was interesting.

Something worth mentioning here is that dogs have a dog language, which they all know how to speak from birth. Take, for example, huskies, who never shut up from the moment they are born. But when a dog loves a human, they can also understand that human's language, even if they've only just met.

And those voices Nugget had been hearing were, in fact, human. They belonged to the Vandycks, and Nugget loved them from the moment he met them. In the weeks that followed, as the puppies graduated from crawling to walking to following the Vandycks around their home, Nugget's love for his humans only grew.

The Vandycks lived in Dorchester, a sprawling, tree-lined neighborhood on the south side of Boston. Specifically, they lived at 99 Ichabod Lane in a little blue house hidden behind a hydrangea hedge. Mr. Vandyck was a businessman who went to work every day in a suit and tie, came home, and immediately changed into jeans and a T-shirt bearing the name of some old rock band. Then he'd go to the sound system, put on a record by whatever band he was wearing that day, call out "Wendy!" and wait patiently for Nugget's mother to lumber over so he could scratch her behind the ears while he mused on what to make for dinner that night and how much counter space he had to work with.

The counters were constantly full because Mrs. Vandyck was a professional baker who always filled the house with amazing smells, working on new recipes for cookies, cupcakes, and other treats. Unfortunately, she was also always placing those treats on surfaces far too high for Nugget and his siblings to reach.

"It's a crime," said Bacon, peering into the kitchen from around the corner.

"It's an accident," said Nugget. "It has to be. If she knew how badly we wanted to eat the cupcakes, she would obviously leave them on the floor. She's a nice lady. She just doesn't know."

"Ignorance of the law is no excuse," said Cheese Fries, who had discovered TV this week.

"We should just tell her," Sprite said. "On three, let's all ask her politely but firmly to reconsider her actions. One . . . two . . . *three!*"

At which point all free-roaming, opinionated puppies were promptly rounded up by Mrs. Vandyck and ushered back into their nest. This happened about once a day.

But no human held a higher place in Nugget's heart than Taylor Vandyck. Taylor was twelve years old, bright-eyed, tall for her age, and an astoundingly easy girl to love. First off, she had given Nugget his name, and Nugget liked his name, and when someone gives you a gift like that, you're inclined to love them forever. On top of that, Taylor was kind and warm and quick to laugh when you licked her face, which was always a nice quality for a friend to have.

But what really sealed the deal—what made Nugget feel that love so strongly it made every inch of his fur stand on end—was the Pattern.

3

The Pattern

The Pattern started just before spring of that year, a couple weeks into Nugget being alive. Well, possibly it had started before then. But that was when Nugget's ears started to turn from puppy ears into dog ears, capable of hearing things thousands of feet away.

That was how, at 3:00 p.m. every day, he started to hear it: a *slap, slap, slap,* always beginning far in the distance before quickly growing closer. And as it grew closer, it grew louder. And as it grew louder, a smell became clearer, blowing on the wind, a scent like grass stains, laughter, and vanilla. And as the smell became clearer, the sound grew faster and louder still, until it all reached a fever pitch: *slap, slap, slap, SLAP—SLAM!*

At this point the Vandycks' front door would fly open, two objects would smack against the foyer wall like they'd been thrown at high speed, and a voice would ring out: "I missed you guys!"

The Pattern was the sound of Taylor Vandyck rushing back from school—not walking, but running as fast as she possibly could—every single day, so that she could kick her sneakers off with wild abandon and find the puppies she'd been thinking about since 7:00 that morning. Once she'd reached the nest in the back of the house, she would get down on the floor with them and let them know how excited she'd been all day to play.

How could you not love a girl like that?

It wasn't long before Taylor could tell Nugget and his siblings apart much better than Mr. or Mrs. Vandyck could. She knew that Biscuit had white ears and a black nose, but that Pepper had black ears and a white nose. She knew that Frosty and Bacon loved playing tug-of-war, but that, depending on who lost, Frosty could be salty and Bacon could be frosty. She knew that when Sprite got excited, she could wag her tail so hard she knocked herself over, and that somehow it was the chronically dozy Cheese Fries that always got caught underfoot, so you had to look out for her. And she knew that Nugget was the one who looked—

Well, actually, we should probably stop and talk about how exactly Nugget looked.

4

How Nugget Looked

It would be very easy to tell you how Nugget and his siblings looked, if only Nugget and his siblings had been any particular breed of dog. If they'd been Weimaraners, you could simply read the sentence "Nugget and his siblings were Weimaraners," and then go look up *Weimaraner* on the internet and say to yourself, "Oh, I see. They looked like that." Or, if you happen to own a Weimaraner, you could go into the living room, look at them very intently, and then say to yourself, "Yes, just as I remembered."

But in this case, it wasn't that simple. For one thing, Wendy was already a canine of indeterminate origin. She was a big black dog with white paws, a thick snout, and a curiously curly tail. Once, the Vandycks had a DNA test done, hoping it might tell them what kind of dog Wendy was. The woman who processed and returned the test included a note congratulating them. In all her years of canine research, she said, she'd never seen a test where so many of the results were just question marks.

Then there was the matter of paternity. If anyone knew

the breed of the puppies' father, then they may have known at least 50 percent of what Nugget and company were. But no one even knew *who* the father was, let alone what he looked like. The only member of the Vandyck household who had met him was Wendy herself; and though the puppies would occasionally ask Wendy about his identity, more often than not, she would just smile a private half smile and not say a word. (We'll come back to this.)

So Nugget and his siblings weren't Weimaraners. Or if they were, they were only Weimaraners the same way a hot fudge sundae is only maraschino cherries—there's a little bit of that ingredient in there, yes, but there's also a whole lot of everything else.

So it's going to require a bit more effort to tell you how Nugget looked.

One easy way to describe a dog's appearance is often its size, but given that he was a puppy, Nugget's size was less of a fixed fact and more of an ongoing news story with frequent, and frequently baffling, updates. It was anyone's guess as to whether the puppies would end up being as big as their mother, or twice as big, or half her size. Some of them were growing faster than the others. (Pepper in particular was really going for it, and her rapid growth made her the envy of her siblings one and all.) Nugget, though, was growing slowly compared to his siblings—with a couple notable exceptions. Nugget's ears appeared to have made a private agreement, early on, that they would race each other to see which of them could grow bigger fastest. Failing that, they would team up against the rest of Nugget's body and make a mad dash to outgrow the whole package.

So we have our first rough sketch of Nugget: a tiny, inquiring face, framed by two large, silky-soft ears that, if Nugget ran fast enough, threatened to send him tumbling over his similarly outsized paws by flopping up and down over his deep brown eyes.

Which brings us to another trait: coloration. As previously discussed, Wendy was black with white paws, and Pepper and Biscuit carried on proudly in their mother's likeness, mixing up black and white in a furry free-for-all of spots and specks. From there, things grew gradually less easy to keep track of: Frosty was almost entirely white, with a black spot that seemed to be growing. Sprite was almost entirely black, with a white spot that seemed to be shrinking. Bacon's and Cheese Fries' black spots were outlined by streaks of russet red that had to have come from either their mysterious father or some long-forgotten red wolf forefather. And by the time you got to Nugget, any sort of strict color scheme had fallen apart altogether. Everything from Nugget's giant ears to the tip of his tail was an eye-catching explosion of black, white, dark orangey-red, light reddish-orange, and—in the case of one streak that ran right down the middle of Nugget's nose—brown, a rich, radiant shade that shone in a sunset's light and brought out the beautiful brown in Nugget's eyes.

Okay. We're getting closer. Brown eyes peeking out from behind big ears, on top of big paws, surrounded by coronas of color. You now almost know what Nugget looked like. But there is more to knowing someone's appearance than knowing how they look. There is also the matter of how they *appear*.

For example: Nugget's eyes may have *looked* brown, but they *appeared* inquisitive, curious, always looking up at what his mother or the Vandycks were doing, all the better for him to learn how to do it too, how to help, how to show the people he loved that he wanted to be just like them.

Nugget may have *looked* small, but he *appeared* mighty, energized, and animated by an excitement for everything around him that caused his paws to bounce clear off the ground and inspired his hindquarters to wag back and forth so fast his tail began to neither look *nor* appear like anything so much as a colorful blur.

And Nugget may not have *looked* like any particular breed previously recorded in anyone's particular breed book. But he did *appear* to be one specific thing, a thing he was reminded of over and over in his first few weeks of life, a thing he'd been hearing since the same breath in which he'd been given his very name.

Because, according to all available experts on the subject, Nugget was *cute*.

Taylor Vandyck had cried it out involuntarily when Nugget was born. Dr. Sheynberg, the veterinarian, had said it in a laugh when Nugget had wriggled and sneezed at his first vaccinations. And either one or both of the Vandyck parents had said it the day Nugget had first ventured out onto the front porch.

It was hard to remember who had said it first that day; in that moment, Nugget had been a little overstimulated. Walking was a relatively new concept at that point, and while he'd pieced together the basic concept of the outdoors from various glimpses and smells, it was still more of a theory to Nugget than a practice. On top of all that, the hydrangea hedge was in full bloom that week, and when the sweet smell of those gigantic flowers first crashed into him, it was with a force that knocked Nugget onto his back. As the Vandycks wiped tears of laughter from their eyes, Nugget wiggled all four paws in the air and waggled his tail furiously, looking for all the world like a deliriously happy overturned turtle. And all the while, there was that oft-heard word: *cute*.

"That's what breed you are, Nugget," Mrs. Vandyck had announced once she'd bent down and helped flip Nugget the right way up again. "Cute. Your breed is just *cute*."

And the other Vandycks had nodded and smiled and agreed never to bring up the question of breed again. Not that it had ever really mattered, but in any case, now it had been decisively solved.

Up till then, Nugget had never particularly cared what he looked like. Neither had he intentionally gone out of his way to be considered cute. But something fell into place in those moments: It was good, Nugget decided, to be cute. It made people happy, and that made *Nugget* happy, and therefore, it could only be good.

And soon enough, Taylor realized that this was something that set Nugget apart from his siblings: his desire to be told when he was being cute. Every time it happened, Nugget would light up with delight and hurl himself into Taylor's lap to celebrate, which she of course loved, which of course only inspired her to call him cute again. It would even have been tempting to say it was Nugget's favorite thing in the world, but it wasn't. Taylor knew, and all Nugget's family knew, that his favorite thing in the world was just to spend time with his family. "Cute" was nice, but at the end of the day, Nugget was happy simply to have a friend who made room in her busy twelve-year-old's schedule to spend time with him. Time with the people he loved was the greatest gift Nugget could get.

He didn't know this yet, but he would not get much more time at all.

Not with these people anyway.

So it was nice that he was getting it now at least.

Sorry.

5

That Thing We Said We'd Come Back To

Nugget's time with the Vandycks was almost up.

But first, one more happy memory, and one more note on family.

Most days, Nugget didn't particularly think about his father, or lack thereof. With seven canine family members and three humans to keep track of, Nugget already had more family under one roof than many humans *or* dogs ever did.

But some days, you just couldn't *not* think about it. Some days, you'd catch a strong smell on the wind and run to the front window to see a glimpse of not one but *two* dogs walking past, their same-but-slightly-different scents just *screaming* "father and son," and then (over the sound of Sprite yelling, "Hi! Hi! Hi! We're here in the house! Hi! Can you hear me? I'll speak louder! Hi!") Mrs. Vandyck would say, "Oh, there go the Ellsworths, walking Buster and Buster Jr. Aren't they cute?" and Mr. Vandyck would mutter, "Yes, though they could've been more creative with the names," and Sprite would continue, "Hi! Hi! H— Oh, they're gone. That's okay, we'll talk next time."

Other days, Taylor would come down from her room just before dinner, her normally bright eyes swollen up with tears, devastated by a conversation with a classmate that hadn't gone the way she expected it to or by the ending of a book that very much *had* gone the way she expected it to but had still made her terribly sad. On days like those, Mr. Vandyck would drop whatever dinner plans he'd been working on, even if he'd already chopped up all the vegetables. He would put them away and tear open a little blue box of bright yellow mac and cheese. Then he would let Taylor stir the cheese into the pot while she talked about whatever had happened that day, or else just leaned on her father's shoulder and didn't talk at all, as Nugget and any number of his siblings tossed and tumbled around Taylor's ankles, imploring her not to be sad, to remember she was loved, and to maybe, while she was at it, possibly find it in her heart to drop a few pieces of cheese.

On days like those, Nugget couldn't help it—he wondered what it would be like to have a father. He tried not to let it worry him, but it was a big question, and Nugget still had a small body, and while his body was still growing, some days the question grew faster.

Until finally, when Nugget was eight or nine weeks old, he couldn't keep it inside anymore and went in search of answers.

Answers were found lying in front of a food bowl marked WENDY, contentedly munching on a mouthful of kibble.

"Hey, Mom," Nugget said. "Can I ask a question?"

Wendy didn't get up, but she did finish her chewing, swallow her food, and smile her soft half smile.

"Not only *can* you ask a question," she said, "you just *did*."

That made Nugget laugh. Then he remembered how big his question was, and grew serious again.

"Okay," he said. "Well, I just wanted to know . . . I mean, I was wondering . . . that is, I thought . . ."

Nugget stopped, started, stopped again. For a moment it looked like Wendy was going to take another bite of food to give Nugget time to think, and that made him blurt his words out as fast as he could, just to get it over with: "Is it weird that I don't have a dad? Would we be a complete family if we had a mom and a dad? Like how Taylor has Mr. and Mrs. Vandyck?"

Instantly, Nugget felt silly. He didn't want to seem ungrateful for everything his mother did for him and his siblings. For the past two months she had fed them, cleaned them, and kept them cuddled close at night. Nugget knew that he had an incredible mom, and he hoped his question in no way suggested otherwise.

But to her credit, Wendy considered the question seriously. She laid her head down on one paw, before taking a moment to try out the other. Finally, after a few moments' solemn contemplation, she raised her head back up to look right at Nugget.

"Yes," she said. "We would be a complete family. But we're also a complete family now. Family isn't a checklist you have to cross off. It's just the people you choose, who choose you back."

And then, with a speed that belied her large and gentle nature, Wendy leaped up and pinned a squealing Nugget to the floor.

"And I," she said, licking over Nugget's helpless laughter, "am so glad you chose me, so that I got to choose you back."

For such a big conversation, it happened surprisingly quickly. But like many things that happen quickly, it shaped the rest of Nugget's life.

From that day forward, Nugget knew that his family didn't have to look like any one thing, because family was who he chose. Like when he chose to cheer up Taylor after a bad day, or when Mrs. Vandyck chose to let him have, okay, just *one* mini-cupcake made with dog-safe ingredients.

And so those became the pillars of Nugget's young life: choosing his family, and trusting they would choose him back. But—just as a backup policy, just to really up the odds that they always *would* choose him back—Nugget always made sure to be very, very cute.

Alright. That was the one more happy memory.

Now for the unhappy one.

6

The Pillars Come Down

One day, Mrs. Vandyck was working on a new batch of mini-doughnuts. Most of the puppies were running around the backyard, engaging in a diplomatic skirmish with the family of squirrels next door. Nugget, however, was inside. He sat in the kitchen, staring closely at Mrs. Vandyck's every move. He was testing out an unfounded but optimistic theory that mini-doughnuts might be meant for mini-dogs.

This was why Nugget was there to see Mrs. Vandyck get the phone call.

"Hey! How are you?" she said.

Then: "Oh."

Then: "Okay," and then, "Right," and then, "I know. I guess I just . . . right. Okay. I love you. See you soon."

Mrs. Vandyck hung up the phone, leaned on the counter, and joined Nugget in staring at her mini-doughnuts.

She did this for several minutes.

Then she promptly set about doubling the size of her batch.

When Taylor returned from school that day, Mrs.

Vandyck tried to get her attention. But Taylor, sprinting with the winged ankles of the Pattern, just waved at her mother and chirped, "Hi, Mom—can't talk—puppies outside—hi, Nugget, bye, Nugget—bye, Mom!" At which point she disappeared again out the back door, leaving Mrs. Vandyck alone in the kitchen with Nugget and a small mountain range of mini-doughnuts.

Mr. Vandyck came home from work shortly after that, but he did not change into a T-shirt. He went to the kitchen, but he didn't start opening cookbooks, or chopping up vegetables, or even clearing up counter space amid the now frankly alarming amount of baked goods. He just went straight to the pantry and got out the little blue box.

As far as Nugget was concerned, this was shaping up to be a great day. Taylor was about to get her favorite comfort food and she didn't even seem to need any comforting. And at least *one* of those doughnuts had to be headed for the floor sooner or later. When Taylor came in from the backyard and lit up at the smell of mac and cheese, her joy seemed to confirm Nugget's feelings: It was a banner day in the Vandyck household.

But with a sigh, Mr. Vandyck gave Taylor her bowl of mac and cheese and asked her to sit at the table.

"I've been offered a new position at work," Mr. Vandyck said, once all three humans (and at least one canine onlooker) were seated.

Taylor, who had been dropping some extra Monterey Jack into her bowl, looked up and beamed.

"You got the promotion you wanted?" she asked. "That's great!"

Mr. and Mrs. Vandyck looked at each other.

"Yes," said Mr. Vandyck. "It is. I've wanted this for a long time, and I honestly didn't even expect to get it. But . . . the position. It's in San Francisco."

The table fell silent except for the squishy sounds of Taylor stirring her mac and cheese, pulling out a steaming spoonful, taking a bite, and chewing thoughtfully.

Her parents studied her.

Nugget studied her spoon.

At last, Taylor swallowed.

"So we're moving," she said.

"Yes," said Mrs. Vandyck. "You'll be able to finish the school year, but we'll need to leave pretty quickly after that. We're so sorry, Taylor. We know you love your friends here, and—"

But Taylor held up a hand.

"No," she said. "I mean—no, you don't have to be sorry. Dad said this might happen last spring, so I've had a lot of time to think about it. And honestly, the timing couldn't be better. Most of my friends are going to a different high school than me next year anyway. If I'm going to have to make new friends, I might as well do it somewhere cool. And *San Francisco*? Come *on*! That's *so* cool! Way to go, Dad!"

Mr. and Mrs. Vandyck looked at each other again. This time, though, their shared expression had changed from dread to pleasant astonishment.

"That's an incredibly mature attitude to take," said Mrs. Vandyck.

"How did we get so lucky?" Mr. Vandyck added, grinning with relief. "And, Taylor—if you want to talk about this further in any way, we'll absolutely be here for you. But, gosh. You really are just an incredible kid, huh?"

"*Sho* true," Taylor agreed through a mouthful of pasta. "I'm *alwaysh* shaying thish."

The Vandycks laughed. Buoyed by their contagious joy, Nugget wagged his tail back and forth across the tile floor. This caused Taylor to look down at him, which caused her smile to light up even brighter.

"And just think!" she said. "The puppies are going to *love* it."

The room fell silent again.

Taylor looked back up at her parents.

They were no longer laughing.

And the pillars of Nugget's world came tumbling down.

7

A House Divided

"We *have* to take them!"

Dogs, as you by now know, have incredible hearing.

"I wish we could, Taylor. We both do."

They can hear you mention their name, even if you say it from behind a closed door or even if they're a floor below you.

"You already expected me to give up all my friends at school, and I said *yes*! But to give *them* up? How *could* you?"

Two floors, if you say it while opening a fridge.

"We'll still be taking Wendy. We just can't take all of them. We were *never* going to be able to care for eight fully grown dogs, Taylor, even if we didn't move. We were going to put up ads soon. You *must* have known this was going to happen. It's just that now we'll have to get rid of them a little sooner—"

"Get *rid* of them?!"

So you can only imagine as a dog how incredibly easy it is to hear three people arguing about you, on the same floor as you, at full volume. You couldn't ignore it even if you wanted to.

Even if you really, *really* wanted to.

Nugget whimpered as Taylor slammed her hands on the table, pushing herself up and out of her seat. Bacon, Pepper, Biscuit, Frosty, Cheese Fries, and Sprite all watched from the screen door, drawn first by the smell of food and then by the sound of yelling. Fourteen eyes flipped back and forth between each human as they spoke. And Wendy just lay in front of her food bowl, her expression inscrutable as always.

"That was poor phrasing," Mr. Vandyck admitted. "Maybe we should have talked about this more. I got nervous about the promotion, so I didn't mention it much, and I apologize for that. But—"

Taylor was already shaking her head.

"No, no, no, no. Don't you love them?"

"We love them very much," Mrs. Vandyck said, her voice shaking with passion. "That's why we want to do what's responsible for them and find them a good home. And that's not going to be a cramped apartment in the middle of a strange city. And we certainly don't want to send them to some overburdened animal shelter."

"Honestly, Taylor . . ." said Mr. Vandyck, and Nugget smelled trepidation in the air as Mrs. Vandyck cut him a warning look. But it was too late; he was already saying it. "You were being so *reasonable* before—"

"Oh, *I'm* sorry!" Taylor cried out. "I didn't realize it was *unreasonable* to *love*!"

She was crying in earnest now, and now she was running out of the dining room, up the stairs, and into her room, as signaled by the *SLAM!* of her bedroom door being thrown shut behind her.

The Vandycks were too stunned to move. The puppies were locked out behind the screen door. And Wendy was not movement prone at the best of times.

Everything fell to Nugget.

In an instant, he was up off the floor, skittering away from the table so fast that he slid three feet on the tile. He regained his balance just in time for the staircase—and he needed it. Each carpeted step was at least as tall as Nugget himself. Right now, though, Nugget didn't care. He threw himself up each step, hind legs coiling and uncoiling like springs, front paws reaching out to dig claws into carpet. Soon he was at the top of the stairs and bolting down the hall, only stopping when he reached the one closed door on the second floor. There he pawed and scratched and whimpered at the wood in front of him, until at last it opened to reveal a tearstained Taylor.

Taylor looked down and saw Nugget looking back up at her.

She had no words.

To be fair, neither did Nugget.

At first, they both cried together in Taylor's bed. Soon, though, Nugget realized it was no good for them *both* to cry; he was here to cheer Taylor up. So instead he licked her face until, against all odds, Taylor started to giggle, spluttering through her sobs.

Hello, those licks said. *Don't worry. I'm here for you. You're safe. It's okay.*

Family is who you choose. You chose me.

I choose you back.

Soon, Taylor was laughing so hard that Nugget relinquished his licking campaign momentarily, if only to give her a chance to breathe. Taylor, panting and exhausted from two separate emotional peaks in nearly as many minutes, rolled over and smiled ruefully at Nugget, her eyes still red.

"They're right, you know," she whispered, like she was confessing a secret. "I *did* know this was going to happen. Sort of. I guess. It's just that *knowing* something and *feeling* something are two different things. And when they told me at the table . . . I felt it *all*. And it felt so *sudden*. You know?"

Honestly, Nugget wasn't sure he did know. This was a lot to process. Frankly, he was sort of still processing being alive.

But for Taylor, he was willing to learn.

They fell asleep snuggled up together. Just before he sank into sleep, a single thought fluttered through Nugget's head: *This is all we need to be okay. This time together.*

And at least for the next few days, that's what they had. The Vandyck household settled back into a state of equilibrium. Taylor played with the puppies. The puppies played with one another. Whenever possible, Nugget crept back up to Taylor's bedroom at night, spending as much time with her as he could.

Then, one morning, they woke to the sound of the doorbell.

The new families had arrived.

They were out of time.

8
Early Adopters

"I thought you were going to post ads online!" Taylor shouted at her mother from the bedroom door. Downstairs, Mr. Vandyck was making pleasant conversation with the prospective puppy buyers, leading them to the back of the house.

"We did," Mrs. Vandyck said softly. "People responded very fast. I'm so sorry."

Nugget could smell that Mrs. Vandyck's apology was genuine. But apologies weren't helping Taylor, and they certainly weren't helping Nugget. Before either of the humans could stop him, Nugget burst out from beneath Taylor's feet, running through the open door and down the stairs. He was getting better at this running thing, but he was still small, and he barely managed to squeeze past Mr. Vandyck and the strange new humans before they all arrived at the back of the house.

There, cuddled up together in their spacious puppy cage, were Nugget's siblings. At the sight of Nugget, the puppies all leaped up from their pile to greet him (save Cheese Fries, who continued snoring with aplomb). At ten weeks old, the puppies no longer really needed to nest together—the door to the cage wasn't even closed—but it was nice to be close to your family.

And if Nugget didn't do something, soon they might lose that closeness forever.

"Nugget!" said Bacon. "There you are! Who are these people?"

"They're new families," Nugget panted, his tongue lolling out from the exertion. "They're coming . . . to try . . . and split us up. They don't know what we really want!"

"Aw, they're so happy to see each other!" said one of the strangers, a woman with long red hair. "They're so cute! I just want to tell them how cute they are all day!"

Nugget did his best to ignore this.

"Split us up?" Sprite scoffed. "Not likely. We just have to be clear and firm about our preference to stay together. We got this. I love you guys."

"I love you too," Nugget said. "All of you."

Then the redheaded woman held out a fistful of biscuits.

"Then again," Sprite said, immediately turning toward the woman, "maybe we should consider this issue more rationally."

The rest of the day continued much like that.

"These ones seem nice," Frosty whispered to Bacon as a couple of humans brought in a giggling frizzy-haired child.

"Don't say that!" Nugget hissed. "They're trying to tear us apart!"

"We'd really love to keep them together," said the tallest human to Mr. Vandyck.

"Ignore that," Nugget said.

"Of course," Mr. Vandyck replied. "We'd hate to tear them apart. Our dream is to keep as many of them together as possible."

"That's our dream too! Could we take three to the same home? We have a *huge* yard."

"That would be great!"

"Ignore all of this!" Nugget wailed, but Frosty and Bacon were already nuzzling the child's hands.

"You're so big!" one human cooed at Pepper a few hours later.

"Why, yes, I am," Pepper said, having woken up somewhere between the fourth and fifth visiting family. "Thank you for noticing! You're very big too! And have excellent taste!"

And so on. By the end of the day, one family or another had expressed interest in every single puppy—and, more often than not, the puppies had expressed interest back.

Nugget, though, held firm. While multiple families swooned over his colorful coat or his big silky ears, Nugget hung back at the edge of the cage. While his siblings played and preened for their visitors, Nugget refused to approach anyone, no matter how many treats they held out in their hands. He just sat and glowered and wondered where his mother was.

When night came and the humans had left, six out of seven puppies collapsed together in a heap, tuckered out from the hard work of being adored all day. Nugget remained awake, lying apart from his siblings and glaring at the door, daring it to open, prepared to give a piece of his mind to whichever human had the audacity to enter the room next.

The door opened.

Taylor stepped into the room.

She approached the nest, wrapping her fingers quietly around the top of the cage, and squatted down close to the floor. Her gaze moved tenderly across the sleeping, swelling pile of puppies, before coming to rest on Nugget. She seemed surprised to find him awake—but then she smiled an odd smile.

Her knuckles squeezed white around the cage. "I love you all so much," she whispered.

Nugget didn't want to wake his siblings, but he approached the cage and bucked his nose gently against it, trying to find Taylor's fingers through the wire. *I love you too! We can fight this! We—*

"So maybe this is for the best."

Taylor fell back into a sitting position, as if exhausted by the confession.

Nugget fell away from her too, but it wasn't because he was tired. It was because his world had just moved under him. It was the same feeling he'd gotten the first time his mother had turned away from him as a newborn puppy. But Nugget was much bigger now—and so was the feeling.

"Wendy doesn't need much exercise," Taylor continued. "But you guys . . . you need—you *deserve*—the world. And I care about you too much to keep that from you. I care so much, I wish I could stop caring. But I don't know how."

Taylor either couldn't think of what to say next, or she couldn't bring herself to say it. Instead, she ran her hand over Nugget's brown nose one more time. Nugget, despite himself, wrinkled up his eyes and wagged his tail two times at the familiar touch.

"Just like you don't know how to stop being cute," Taylor sighed with a smile.

And then she got back up on her feet, taking one last look down at the nest.

And then she was gone.

Nugget sat and stared at the door she had left through.

It was a sign of how stunned Nugget was that he did this for several minutes before realizing Taylor had left the door wide open.

9
Next Steps

Nugget didn't know the big, dramatic thing he was going to do next.

He wouldn't know until after he'd done it.

Actually, he wouldn't do the big, dramatic thing for another three minutes (but he didn't know that yet) (because he hadn't done it).

For now, all he'd done was nose his way out of the cage and trot aimlessly out the door—where he had run immediately into Wendy, who was lying down just outside the nest room. It was the first time Nugget had seen her all day.

"Oh, hello, darling," Wendy mumbled, slowly waking up. "Is everything okay?"

"Is everything— *No!*" Nugget knew his mother could be hard to read, but he'd never expected her to be so emotionless in the face of losing her children. "Where have you *been* today?"

Wendy yawned.

"I was giving you space," she said. "We're all going to be moving soon, and we won't all be moving together. I've prepared you all for the world as best as I can. Now I need to prepare you for change."

"But *why*?" Nugget cried. "Why should things change at all? Aren't we a family? Weren't things good? Wasn't *I* good? Wasn't . . ."

Nugget wished he could stop himself from asking what he asked next, but he couldn't. So instead he just asked it as softly as possible, like it wouldn't be as shameful if it couldn't be heard.

"Wasn't I cute enough?"

But mothers can always hear when their children need help, even if they don't have canine-enhanced superhearing. (Though it helps a bit if they do.)

With that same surprising swiftness as before, Wendy shifted her bulk, and suddenly Nugget was trapped warmly between her two front paws. Wendy fixed her son with an intense gaze.

"I hope you don't think your cuteness is what gives you value," Wendy said. "What gives you value is the way you love. I think maybe that's why this is harder for you than any of the others. You were born first. You've loved the longest and the hardest. You've gotten very, very good at it."

"Then why isn't it *enough*?" Nugget asked, unable to hold his questions back any longer. "I love everyone here. Why don't they love me back?"

"They do. Don't you see? The way Taylor fought for

you. The way her father wants to make sure you have a big spacious home with a yard. They're two different ways of showing love."

"And what's your way?" Nugget asked angrily. "Just sitting there while your kids leave you?"

He expected Wendy to say something angry back, but instead Wendy just smiled her mysterious half smile. Then and there, Nugget realized something else about his mother. Before this, he'd assumed that his mom's half smile meant she was only feeling things half as intensely as anyone else. But now Nugget wondered if he'd had it all wrong: Could his mother's half smile be hiding feelings so strong that she couldn't even express them? Could his mother have felt, somehow, *twice* as much as anyone else?

It may not have looked that way, or even appeared that way.

But appearances could be deceiving.

Then Wendy surprised Nugget again.

"This happened to me too, you know," she said. "When I was your age. I loved my mom, and she loved me, but when the Vandycks came, and my mother saw how amazing they were, she knew it was time to let me go. At the time, I didn't understand. Now, though . . . I've had a wonderful life. I do understand. I loved my family then, and I love my family now. Both can be true."

In that moment, Nugget may not have wanted to admit

it, but there was a chance—a small, slight, annoying, unbe-
lievable *chance*—that what his mother was saying made sense.

But then she said one more thing: "And anyway—what
would you have me do?" Wendy asked, her voice gently teas-
ing. "Run away with you on the streets? No, thanks. I'm
too old."

And Nugget got a big, dramatic idea.

"Maybe," he said. "But maybe I'm not."

There was nothing halfway about the look of concern on
Wendy's face that followed. In an instant, she had leaped to
her feet.

"Wait," she said. "Nugget, no. That's not—"

But it was her standing up that made it possible. Nugget,
still the runt of the litter, was just small enough to dash right
between Wendy's four legs and out of the room.

The Vandycks had decided not to choose him? Well,
Nugget could do that right back. Instead of choosing them, he
would choose every step he took next, every big galloping step
that took him away from his family and away from the love so
big that it hurt. Instead he would run down the hall, and out
the doggy door, past the hydrangea hedge that surrounded 99
Ichabod Lane, and out into the night.

Nugget didn't know he was leaving his old life behind
until after he'd done it.

10

Outside

It feels wise to take a moment here to caution against running away from home as a long-term solution to one's problems. In the long term, running away from home often isolates you from the people whose help you need most. In the long term, running away from home can be difficult and dangerous. In the long term, running away from home can even be deadly.

Those are all true—in the long term.

In the short term, Nugget was simply too busy to care.

Worried about the future? Heartbroken over his seeming rejection at the hands of those he loved most? Not Nugget! Not anymore! He simply didn't have *time*! There was so much world to explore, to see, and, most important, to *smell*. Past the hydrangea hedge there was a neighborhood, smelling of freshly mowed grass; just-developing dew; the sodium vapor of buzzing streetlights; the chlorine of a backyard pool. Past the neighborhood, there were railroad tracks smelling of well-traveled iron, the copper tang of flattened pennies, and a family of ducks that had waddled over the rails just a couple hours ago. And past the tracks, there was a long avenue winding away forever to the north and the south and smelling of . . .

Everything.

Dorchester Avenue ran all the way from the outer rings of Boston to the city's beating heart. It was lined with parked cars, car parks, *park* parks, plant life, libraries, locksmiths, churches, temples, restaurants featuring food from all the farthest reaches of the world, and grocery stores selling everything from everywhere in between. For Nugget, it was like an amusement park ride of amazing new scents pulling him from one block to the next. Here he stopped in front of a storefront to drool at a rotisserie chicken. There he lingered by a gas station to inhale the heady scent of gasoline, the faintest whiff of which was enough to blow his big ears back. But nowhere did Nugget linger as long, or as longingly, as in the parks, the soccer fields, the *grass.* Because anything green in Boston didn't just smell like itself.

It smelled like dogs, dogs, *dogs.*

Dogs who had just walked by. Dogs who had stopped to say hello. Dogs who had stopped to say hello and also, "I own this tree now." Trees, in general, were especially intoxicating; they dropped floral scents from above, Japanese snowbell and black locust flowers landing on top of Nugget's nose, while at the same time, from below, their trunks and roots spoke of all who had passed by before or made a claim to ownership (and every square foot of green that Nugget smelled had seemingly been through *many* claims of ownership). Nugget wasn't quite ready to dive into the world of real estate acquisition, but he said hi a few times to be friendly.

Then he kept moving. Because if Nugget didn't keep moving, he might slow down, might lose momentum, might miss something that he could be seeing for the first time ever *right now*.

He might also have to think about everything he had just left behind. And everyone. And how scary that all was.

But mostly Nugget tried to focus on the exciting exploring part.

With the kind of inexhaustible energy found only in puppies who haven't done much all day, Nugget ran on through the Boston night, dashing up and down hills, in and out of alleyways, around the edges of baseball diamonds and then straight across them, like he was stealing second base with no one around to stop him. Nugget didn't know what stealing second base meant, but he loved the way the dirt kicked up around his paws, loved that here was one more new thing for him to find and catalog and assume he would come to understand later.

For a short, wild while the night belonged to Nugget.

Then came the long term.

The first pink streaks of dawn were just bleeding over the eastern rooftops of Dorchester when Nugget trotted out of a park, across a quiet street, and smack-dab onto what had to be the best-smelling sidewalk in Boston. The air was saturated with a scent that set Nugget's heart racing—a scent he knew like the back of his paw.

Someone was baking.

Several someones, in fact. As Nugget turned to find the source of the smell, he saw a wide plate glass window and, through it, several humans dressed in white. They moved back and forth behind a counter, loading trays in and out of an oven.

Nugget knew from Mrs. Vandyck that bakers were some of the earliest risers in any given city. To get a breakfast pastry to someone on their way to work, you needed to be pulling your pastries out of the oven just before rush hour, which meant putting them *in* the oven right at the crack of dawn. Which was right now. And so now, Nugget sat, unaware of the string of drool he had begun to produce, gawking through a window at the first people he had seen since leaving his fami—since leaving Ichabod Lane.

And as had been true all night, when Nugget wasn't running, he was remembering. And the only thing Nugget could remember with sugar and butter thick in the air was the warmth of the Vandycks' kitchen. Did Mrs. Vandyck have anything delicious planned for her baking this morning? If Nugget turned around right now, would he make it home in time to find out?

No. Returning home meant admitting he still had a home to return to. Even if he wanted to—even if running away from home suddenly felt much less like the right decision—Nugget could not let himself go back.

Also, and more importantly: Nugget could not go back, period.

At this point, it's probably time for a brief note on Boston.

11

A Brief Note on Boston

Some cities, when seen from the sky, are grids; their avenues run neatly up and down and their streets run cleanly right to left. They're easy to navigate no matter how busy or big they get. Other cities have streets that end in tight loops, sending you back to the main road you came from, so that it is more or less impossible to get lost.

Boston is not a grid. Neither is it an organized system of loops.

Boston is sort of like if you took a bunch of spaghetti, dropped it on the floor, messed it up with your shoe a little, and then, deciding that this was not yet enough of a mess, jumped up and down on it with both of your shoes, each of which had different and extremely complicated sneaker tread patterns on its sole. Then if you dropped some meatballs not quite *on* but sort of *near* the spaghetti pile (allowing sauce to splatter everywhere and mess things up further) and said, "Those are also part of Boston, for the record," you would more or less have an idea of what the city looked like. You would also have exactly the can-do attitude so often looked for at the city planning department of Boston City Hall.

It was into this city that Nugget had spent the night running, and it was in this city that he was now thoroughly, hopelessly lost.

Because at some point in the night, Nugget had strayed from Dorchester Avenue—the one long, straight noodle of order in all the city's spaghettish chaos. He hadn't noticed at the time, caught up as he was in his adventure. But after investigating a park in Fields Corner, Nugget had not returned to the big two-way road that would have led him home to safety. Instead he'd taken a wrong turn in the darkness and emerged onto a new road entirely. Then, after following that new path for a while, he'd spotted an enticing playground and run into *another* park—and exited *that* park onto yet another road.

That had been hours ago. By this point, Nugget was nowhere near his safety noodle. Or maybe he was just a block away from it, separated only by a single building obscuring his view like a big pile of Parmesan. (Okay, we're done with the spaghetti thing.)

That was the trouble with Boston: You never really knew if the road you were on would lead to the one you wanted, or to a dead end, or—somehow, defying all known laws of physics and several of public engineering—right back around to itself.

So Nugget couldn't go home, even if he wanted to.

Which he didn't.

And yet.

The air smelled like love and food. Breakfast time was fast approaching, and Nugget did not know where his breakfast was going to come from. And though puppies generally have the energy reserves of nuclear reactors with perky little tails, Nugget had to admit that running away was hard work. His eyes were heavy, his legs were wobbly, and he did not know where he was going to sleep.

And there, Nugget began to realize, lay the problem: When your only goal is running *away*, you soon realize you don't know what to run *toward*.

And then you don't know where you are at all.

So.

Keep that in mind if you're ever in Boston.

12
Anyway, Where Were We?

At this point, Nugget had been hypnotized by the bakery window for quite a while, and his drool string had grown long enough that it was now making first contact with the sidewalk. As if somehow hearing this, one of the bakers inside the building chose that moment to turn around and see the small, unattended dog staring at them from the street.

Nugget stiffened, wondering if he should run. Then he realized: no. This was an opportunity. *This* was where his breakfast would come from.

A combination of conditioning and instinct took over. Nugget drew himself up, stuck out his chin, widened his eyes, fluffed his ears forward. His tail wagged once, twice, small, hopeful. Whether he knew it or not, Nugget was deploying every trick in the hungry-dog book. Some had been learned from hours in the Vandyck kitchen; some were just things that every puppy was born knowing how to do.

And all of them hit the baker with maximum force. He leaned forward on the counter and looked left and right out the window, trying to see if anyone was coming to claim Nugget.

Then he pulled back. Looked at Nugget. Looked at the tray of ham croissants that had just come out of the oven. Looked back at Nugget.

A moment later the door to the bakery was opening, and Nugget was jumping for joy, slobber flying everywhere, as the baker knelt down and held out the first bite of a croissant he had torn into puppy-sized pieces.

"Eat up, okay, dog?" the baker whispered. "My boss'll kill me if he sees me giving away free food, but I couldn't help it. You're just so . . . *cute*."

And Nugget couldn't help it either. His heart swelled with love for the baker. On some level he had thought, as puppies and people so often do after first heartbreak, that he might never love someone again. But no. Here was this man, the dark skin of his forearms dusted with white flour, his fingers covered in crumbs that he graciously let Nugget lick up, and his smile furtive but freely given. You only had to look at him once to know: Some people were still good. Some people were still trustworthy.

And no matter what Nugget's mother had said, it was still very, *very* important to be cute.

The food settled in Nugget's stomach, warm and sustaining, and soon that warmth spread through his body. It reached his paws, it wagged his tail, and it pumped through his heart and up to his head, where the thought appeared unbidden: Maybe *this* was what Nugget had been running toward. Wasn't this man choosing Nugget right now? Choosing to help? Maybe Nugget should do something to show him the feeling was mutual, to show that he chose the baker back— Oh, hold on, the guy was talking.

"So, were you just too little for them to put a collar on yet?" the man asked, scratching Nugget's fur back and forth, his big fingers still hot from the baking trays. "Or do you really not belong to anyone?"

Nugget leaped up, put a paw on each of the man's knees, and wagged like a wind turbine. *Yes! No! Both! I belong to you! I—*

"Oh, well." The man straightened up, removing Nugget's pawholds and letting him drop back down to the sidewalk. "Guess that's for animal control to figure out."

No.

The man stepped back to the bakery and now was holding the door open, waiting for Nugget.

"My boss would *not* want you in here—*total* health code violation—but I can't have you running away before animal control gets here."

Nugget didn't know who or what animal control was. But he knew now, from experience, how it sounded when a person you thought you could trust was about to pawn you off on someone else.

The man looked down at Nugget. From beyond the open

door came a blast of air that smelled like a half acre of heaven had gotten loose. It wrapped Nugget up and reminded him of everything he didn't have.

He was tired.

He was tempted.

He was once more off and running.

"Hey!" the man yelled. "I'm trying to help you!"

But Nugget just ran faster, weaving through the first early pedestrians of the morning, leaping over the bristles of a shop-keeper's broom, and rounding the first corner he came to. Even when he was safely out of the baker's sight, he ran on, allowing himself to become even more lost in the impossible streets of Boston.

He ran over cobblestone, over cement, over weeds and wildflowers. Last night, rocketing around the city had been liberating. Now the sun was officially up, the sidewalks were getting hotter by the hour, and the streets were growing busier by the minute. Some people lit up and smiled when they saw Nugget tearing toward them. Others frowned and yelled out "Hey!" or wondered aloud whose dog Nugget was.

Nugget wondered the same thing.

He also wondered how much longer he could run. For Nugget's sake, something needed to change, and soon.

And then he rounded a corner, and something did.

There, rising up out of a tangle of church spires and char-ity shops, was a park bigger than any of the parks Nugget had seen before, even bigger than the biggest imaginable city block. Where other parks had been lined by scatterings of trees, this one was ringed by dense forest. The whole thing looked so large it could have been a small city itself, and indeed, vast structures rose out of the wild green—a giant stadium. A couple of big brown towers. And, bafflingly, a village of huts and tents from which emanated the strangest collection of smells Nugget had ever encountered in his short but busy life. Each of the smells drifting out of the park was so unexpected and so unlike one another that they didn't just seem to come from another planet—they seemed to come from *every* planet.

Nugget came to a momentary halt, trembling on his feet. With bleary eyes, he squinted across the street at one of the park's many entrances. Maybe he should investigate.

But Nugget was bone tired, and he didn't want mysteries. He just wanted somewhere safe to lie down.

That was when he smelled it.

Just beyond the mysterious village, a hill crested out of the park, standing tall over all of Boston. There, on top of the hill, were what looked like small and crumbling castle walls, overgrown ruins of stone and ivy. This should have qualified as another mystery—why in the world, one might wonder, was there a castle in *Boston?*—but wafting down from the ruins was the smell of something furry, and warm, and big and old, like a gigantic blanket.

As if drawn by a magnet, Nugget felt himself cross the street. He was swallowed up by the forest walls of the park, and soon he was pulling himself up the hill. By the time he reached the hill's peak, he was too tired to keep his eyes open, so he let them fall shut and navigated by smell, following his nose into the heart of the blanket scent. But even with his eyes closed, Nugget could feel his progress, written in the wind and the light on his fur. First the thickening leaves overhead blocked out the sun. Then the castle walls blocked out the rustling of the leaves.

Then the walls converged into a tight little corner, positively reeking of warm furry blanket smell, and Nugget nestled himself up inside it. Warm, for now. Safe, for now.

And there, for the first time since he'd lain in Taylor Vandyck's arms, forty hours and forever ago . . . Nugget fell asleep.

And woke up face-to-face with a monster.

13

Lucky

"Ahh!" yelled Nugget, leaping to his feet.

"Ahh!" yelled the monster, in a high-pitched squeal that sounded like a squeaky toy stepping on a landmine.

The two hurled themselves away from each other, but since they were already huddled in the corner of the stone ruins, they didn't get very far. Nugget and the monster both pressed themselves up against their respective stone wall and panted, staring at each other.

There was a lot for Nugget to stare at.

It was nighttime, but even in the shadows, Nugget could see that the monster was huge—not as big as a human, but easily the size of two or three Nuggets put together. Its body and back were made of nothing but spikes: tall, sharp spikes so long they bent over with their own fierce weight, striped with white and black like war paint, each raised to its maximum height, spread out like an exploding pine cone frozen in time—frozen, but still threatening at any second to break loose and attack. The spikes quivered as the monster made a horrible din, releasing a flood of sounds that were . . .

Well, that were actually . . .

Okay, so the noises the monster made were actually pretty . . . funny. And kind of . . . adorable. And once you looked under the sharp pointy bits, the monster itself wasn't *that* monstrous? *Some* parts looked scary, sure, but others didn't. In some ways, the monster was even—there was no denying it—*cute*. Cute in a different way from Nugget, but nevertheless: stubby little paws; small eyes, scrunched up in adorable indignation; and, dominating everything else, an endearingly honking big nose.

Well, the spikes *really* dominated everything else. But the schnoz was a close second.

As he observed all this, Nugget began to wonder if he hadn't misjudged this creature. After all, it wasn't like the monster was *attacking* him; it was just standing there, squeaking passionately. And as soon as Nugget realized these things, and that this creature might be more lovable than first assumed, all that squeaking began to settle down into something Nugget could hear and understand.

". . . nearly scared the quills offa me! Didn't ya mothah ever teach you any manners?" said the monster, which didn't seem like a very monstrous thing to say at all.

"I'm sorry," Nugget said. "I didn't mean to frighten you. You just frightened—I mean, you *surprised* me. First."

"Oh! He speaks!" The monster bristled—and here was someone who could *really* bristle. "Eish! What's the mattah?

You never seen a porcupine? Or just never seen one this handsome before?"

Nugget considered both questions.

"No," he answered honestly.

The porcupine regarded Nugget suspiciously, and then sighed.

"Yeah," he said. "I get that a lot."

Slowly, the porcupine's spikes—what had he called them? His *quills*—all lowered from their defensive positions, tapering along the beast's body like a slicked-back hairdo (albeit with several extremely pointy flyaways).

"I'm Lucky," said the porcupine. "Howzit?"

"How's what?" Nugget asked, and when it seemed like Lucky was about to start another squeaky tirade, Nugget hurried onward: "Oh, I'm—I'm fine! I'm Nugget. Sorry. I don't mean to be rude, you just have . . . the *strangest* accent."

"Well, one, that *is* rude," Lucky said. "But two, I mean . . . yehr. I'm a South African porcupine, and I was raised by a bunch of Boston zookeepers. You have no idea what that does to your dialect. It's wicked odd, my bru."

This was a lot for Nugget to take in. He decided to tackle one thing at a time.

"Um . . . zookeepers?"

Lucky nodded, which was an arresting sight. The quills were still rippling thirty seconds after the head had stopped moving.

"Yehr, the zookeepers—the people who feed me and wash my enclosure," said Lucky. "And the enclosures for all the other animals in the zoo."

Nugget felt it best to stick with his current approach.

"The . . . zoo?"

"Oh, wow, okay," Lucky said. "So, a *zoo* is like a place where all kinds of different animals come to, so we can hang out and look at humans all day."

By this point, Nugget (who, in his defense, had just woken up two minutes ago) was starting to put a few things together.

"Oh!" he exclaimed. "You mean you're from that village with all the weird smells? And those weird smells . . . are other animals from around the world? That you live with?"

Again, Lucky nodded, and again, his quills wibbled and wobbled.

"It's a living," he said blithely.

After that, Lucky fell silent, taking a moment to fluff out his quills. Either the porcupine was giving Nugget time to process everything, or he was simply not very invested in this conversation.

Nugget, ever the believer in new friends, assumed it was the first option. Frankly, he was grateful. The last time he'd been awake, Nugget hadn't even had his eyes open to see where he'd been walking. Now, in this momentary silence, he was finally able to look around and take in his surroundings.

Upon doing so, he was both horrified and sort of glad

to think he'd first walked through here with his eyes closed. The puppy and the porcupine were surrounded by crumbling stone walls, yes, but that's not all they were surrounded by. The earth around them was marred by wide pits, dug deep into the ground and crammed full of fallen leaves and litter— cans, bottles, boxes, and, in one pit a few yards away, what appeared to be an overturned barbecue grill. The fact that Nugget hadn't fallen into one of these was a miracle—and a relief, considering the pits were lined with sharp iron bars, some of which jutted upward at fearsome angles, and others of which bent downward, ending in sharp spikes, not unlike the spikes on . . .

"Lucky?" Nugget asked, astonished. "Is . . . is this *your* enclosure? Is this part of the zoo?"

"Oh, this?" Lucky looked up from where he had been carefully (very carefully) grooming his quills. "No. My shelter's *way* nicer than this. These are the old bear cages."

Nugget, who had just started feeling relaxed enough to peel himself off the wall, pressed himself right back up against it.

"Bears?!"

"Oh, sure." Lucky rolled his eyes. "Bears, he's heard of. Some animals get all the press."

It was true: Nugget knew about bears. He'd heard about them from Cheese Fries, who had heard about them from watching TV. Bears were big, bigger than humans, and according to the TV, they ate anything that came across their path. Like picnic baskets. Or people. Or worst of all, cute little puppies.

Suddenly the smell that had first drawn Nugget in made a terrible sort of sense. It was furry, yes. It was big. And it was old. But it was *not* the smell of a safe and warm blanket.

It was the smell of a bear's den.

And Nugget had wandered right inside it.

14

Bears

"We have to get out of here!" Nugget cried, bounding frantically one way and then another. Which way had he come in from? And even if he found it, would it be a safe way out? Or was a grizzly bear waiting right around the corner to punish them for intruding on its turf?

And why in the world was Lucky so *calm*?

"Relax, kid," Lucky said, watching Nugget impassively. "It's an *old* bear's den."

"I know! I can smell them! They smell very old!"

"Wow, you can still smell them?" Despite himself, Lucky seemed impressed. "That's some nose you got—and I'm one to. talk. But you're not understanding, my bru. It's not an *old-bear's* den. It's an old *bear's den*. The fine folks at the Franklin Park Zoo stopped using it—or maintaining it, as you can see—long before I ever even came to America. I wander up here at night because sometimes the townie punks leave food here, and also because it's cool. And I'm nocturnal. And bored. But there haven't been any bears here for years and years."

Lucky's words helped Nugget to calm down. For one thing, the porcupine's Boston accent had caused that last sentence to sound more like "Theh haven't been any beahs heeah feh yeeahs and yeeahs," and the energy required for mental translation meant Nugget briefly had to focus on something other than mortal terror. For another thing, he realized it was true: The bear scent may have been slathered all over this place, but it was a scent from long ago, like those trees he had smelled last night, transmitting messages from dogs in the distant past. In the here and now, if he really focused on his sniffing, Nugget could detect much fresher scents: the tang of spray paint, clinging to the walls in the form of colorful graffiti; the sticky spilled soda of teenage humans; and, crisscrossing back and forth through the bear's den like a scribbled little line, the just-acquired but unmistakable smell of porcupine.

"You come *here* to hang out?" Nugget asked, unable to keep the surprise out of his voice.

Lucky shrugged. "I like it," he said. "I know it's not the prettiest place in town, but it's got something better than pretty. It's got *character.*"

"Character?" Nugget tilted his head, looking around, trying to understand.

In the spaces between the leaves overhead, some flickering light managed to make itself known. It swam across a wall, animating a stone carving of two fearsome stone bears, making them look like they were dancing in the moonlight.

"Yehr, character," Lucky said, following Nugget's gaze. "Something authentic. Something unique. Something way better than sitting alone in my little enclosure."

Lucky paused. Then, as if worried he had given too much away, he shook out his quills.

"So imagine my surprise," he went on, "when I arrive tonight and find a tiny little puppy, who can't be more than a few months old, snoring away in the old polar bear den. And I'm just wondering if he needs medical attention when—*eish!* He's barkin' in my face like some kinda attack dog!"

"I'm sorry," Nugget said again. "I was just scared, because—because I'm lost, and I ran away from home, or—or I don't even have a home, really, and I'm just trying to figure out where to live next, and what I'm going to eat."

Lucky considered this. He twitched his big nose to the left, then to the right.

"Ah," he said. "Yehr. That's wicked rough." He turned around, leaving Nugget to narrowly dodge getting a faceful of quill, and started to waddle away. "Wish I could help," the porcupine said. "But good luck! Maybe I'll see ya around!"

Nugget stared open-mouthed at the pile of spikes shambling away from him. In that moment, it was like he was right back at 99 Ichabod Lane, watching Taylor walk out the door. And that temptation arose again to do what he'd done to her, to the baker, to everyone in the past two days—to run away.

But Nugget looked around at the jagged iron bars, and

the mountains of litter, and thought about where running had gotten him so far.

"Wait!" he called out.

Lucky didn't turn around, but his shambling gait came to a halt. (His quills, as always, took a few seconds to follow his lead.)

"I think you *can* help me," Nugget said. "You said you knew where to find shelter? And food? I need help finding both of those things!"

"I said I *have* a shelter," Lucky said. "*And* food. It's brought to me every day, by my zookeepers—my *personal staff*—who, for the record, would probably *not* be happy to find their South African porcupine sharing his enclosure with a North American . . . *whatever* you are. Why should I put myself on the line like that? What do you have to offer in return?"

Nugget wracked his brain for something, anything, to win Lucky over.

It actually didn't take him very long to find an answer. After all, Nugget loved everyone he met, even if they were sort of . . . prickly. And when you love someone, it makes you a very good listener.

"Didn't you say you were lone—I mean, bored?" Nugget asked carefully. "What could be less boring than harboring a secret runaway puppy in your enclosure?"

There was a pause.

Then: the soft rustling of quills as Lucky finally turned his head just enough to look back at Nugget.

"Fine," he said. "I'll take you on for a trial internship. But you do what I say, kid. Stick with me. And don't slow me down!"

And with that, he was waddling off again.

"Thank you, Mr. Lucky! I will! I mean, I won't!" Nugget bounded after Lucky, circling right back when he immediately overtook the slow-moving porcupine. "And, I mean, not to be rude, but you don't walk that fast!"

"Okay, lesson number one," Lucky grunted, ambling around an empty can of spray paint and down the first few steps of a stone stairway. "I know you were born two days ago or whatever, but you gotta stop saying 'not to be rude' and then saying something *wicked* rude."

"Sorry, Mr. Lucky!"

"And just call me Lucky. Mr. Lucky was my fathah."

"Okay, Mr. Lu— Okay!"

And with that, the puppy and the porcupine made their way out of the stone ruins of the abandoned Boston bear cages, down the hill, and toward the lights of the Franklin Park Zoo.

15

The Zoo

The Franklin Park Zoo is over a hundred years old, and Boston's biggest zoo.

It is also Boston's only zoo.

To be honest, it's not really that big.

When the Franklin Park Zoo first opened in 1912, it received millions of visitors every year. In the century since then, however, other zoos were built around the world, many of which had flashier exhibits, bigger budgets, and larger, more sprawling estates.

The Franklin Park Zoo had none of those things, and by the time Nugget arrived, it no longer had millions of visitors.

But it did have two things of interest.

First: It had character.

Second: It had an old fence.

More specifically: At the bottom of an old fence near the northwestern corner of the zoo, it had a small divot of smooth dirt worn away by years of erosion. Between the spacing of the fence and the dipping of the dirt, there was a passageway just barely big enough for a South African porcupine to squeeze in and out, and more than big enough for a small puppy of indeterminate breed to wriggle through, thus allowing said puppy to access an entire globe's worth of exciting new smells.

So the Franklin Park Zoo was, to Nugget's eyes (and his nose), absolutely perfect.

"What's that?" Nugget asked, for the third time in five minutes, whipping his nose left toward a smell like bamboo and brute power.

"That's the gorillas," Lucky said gruffly. "They're not nocturnal. Don't bug 'em."

"Okay!" Nugget filed this knowledge away for later and continued to follow Lucky down the wide, plant-lined promenade between zoo exhibits.

Then: "What's *that*?" Nugget asked, turning right this time, catching a scent like hot clay, baked under the sun of another world.

"Kangaroos. They *are* nocturnal, but don't bug 'em anyway."

"Okay!" And then, a second later, at the strongest smell yet: "Wait, what's *th*—"

Lucky turned to face Nugget.

"First, I am not your tour guide. I am here to take you on the *opposite* of a tour. I am taking you back to my enclosure, where you are going to hide and sleep and avoid getting me in trouble with my zookeepers. That does not involve me showing you around the zoo or telling you what every animal on Earth is. Second, it's a lion. In fact, it's several lions. And I honestly don't even know if the lions are nocturnal or not—I don't get close enough to ask—but we do not. Bug. The lions."

Nugget nodded. This did not seem unreasonable. Cheese Fries had also told him about lions.

Lucky regarded Nugget carefully. When it became clear there were going to be no objections, the porcupine huffed with satisfaction and turned back in the direction they'd been walking.

"Lekker," he said, which appeared to be a good thing. "Now, let's get you to the guest room."

Lucky's guest room turned out to be a hollow log. More accurately, it was slightly less than half a hollow log. Lucky's room was the other, larger log half. The log in question lay in the center of Lucky's enclosure. The enclosure consisted of a rectangular patch of grass bordered on one side by a small zookeepers' hut and on its three other sides by a chain-link fence. The fence was newer than the one around the zoo's perimeter, but there was still a small gap where the chain did not quite link up with the hut, and it was through this gap that Lucky entered his enclosure and then stopped, waiting for his young charge to follow him. The moment Nugget made his way through—and not a moment later—Lucky kicked up a storm of leaves and scrub with his hind legs, creating a pile around the hole in the fence such that any zookeeper with their dull human senses would have been hard-pressed to notice there was even a hole there in the first place.

Beyond that, the only other features inside the grassy enclosure were a few more fallen logs, a red rubber ball, and a small watering station located next to the hut. On the far side of the chain-link fence, Nugget could see—and smell—a pair of large, lumpy creatures, sleeping soundly. Their snores were lent a strange whistling tone by the tusks poking out of their mouths.

"My neighbors, the warthogs," Lucky whispered. "Nice enough folks. A bit boorish. Now let's get you to bed—the sun's coming up, and the sooner you're asleep, the sooner I can stop worrying about you running around and getting me in trouble."

Once again, Nugget had no objections. After two nights in a row of adventure and discovery, he was starting to associate the sunrise with suddenly noticing how tired he was. But before Nugget could step into his half of the log, Lucky huffed again.

"Wait," he said.

Nugget froze. Was this it? Was this the moment when Lucky changed his mind and sent Nugget away like everyone before him?

But Lucky just lumbered into the log and, after a few minutes' shuffling and grumbling, cleared out all the stray sharp quills from the spot where Nugget would be sleeping.

"There," Lucky grunted when he was done. "Don't let anyone say I'm not a good host."

Nugget smiled so big that for a second he thought he might give Lucky some good old-fashioned face licks out of gratitude. In the interest of keeping his tongue unpunctured, he decided against it, but his wagging tail gave away his joy regardless. Lucky saw this, and for a moment, it seemed like he was going to say something.

But then, just as he had done back in the bear's den, he shook out his quills, nodded curtly, and walked away, leaving Nugget to his rest.

It didn't matter. That morning, for the first time in what felt like a long time, Nugget fell asleep with a smile on his face.

16
Log Jam

When Nugget awoke, he once again found himself inches away from Lucky's face.

This time, however, instead of panicking, Nugget just yawned, smiled, and wagged.

Lucky did not smile back.

"Is it nighttime again already?!" Nugget asked, excited to play.

"No. It's the middle of the day." Lucky shifted his stance slightly and revealed that he'd been blocking out the sunlight, which now pierced through the log in spears of bright heat through the spaces between Lucky's quills. And now, as Nugget became more aware of his surroundings, he heard a sound he hadn't processed yet but knew intimately: the laughter of children.

The zoo was officially open for visitors. The air outside was thick with the scent of hot animal fur, cotton candy, and the delight of Boston's families enjoying a beautiful day.

Nugget leaped to his feet, every spark of muscle memory

in his body crackling with the urge: Go! Greet! Play! *Make friends!*

But just before his body won out over his brain, Nugget remembered why exactly Lucky might want to take up so much space in this log: He was blocking the visitors' view of Nugget.

"Right. Yes. You see my problem," Lucky said.

"Sorry, Mr. Lu—Lucky," Nugget said, forcing himself back down onto the cool bark. "But wait—then why did you wake me up?"

"Because," Lucky huffed, "you're making so much *noise*."

"What? I was asleep! Uh-oh. Do I talk in my sleep?"

"It's not your mouth that's the problem, my bru."

Lucky nodded downward.

"It's your stomach."

It was then that Nugget heard the *other* sound he hadn't processed yet: *ggrrrRRrOWLLlleeerp.*

It was loud. It was ferocious. And it was coming from his belly. Nugget, after all, had not eaten anything since yesterday's hasty bakery breakfast. And from the way it was now protesting, this appeared to be an injustice Nugget's stomach would no longer, well, stomach.

"You've been doing that for an hour," Lucky said. "The zookeepers think I have gas."

"I'm sorry!" Nugget cried. "I can't help it! What should

71

I do? Should I eat some bark? Do dogs eat bark? Is that why they call it barking? I'll eat this bark if you—"

"Do *not*," Lucky stressed, "eat my *house*. Only I get to eat my house! Here."

He stood up just long enough to push something forward from under his belly, and then plopped back down again.

"I saved you some of today's lunch," he said.

Nugget looked down at a dazzling, colorful display of different types of dog-friendly fruit.

A quill had gotten stuck on one of the melon cubes.

"Some of it's kebab style," Lucky admitted sheepishly.

But Nugget didn't mind. Far from it.

"Lucky, this is so much food!" he exclaimed. "Is this . . . *all* your lunch?"

Lucky shrugged, clearly growing more uncomfortable by the second. "Only most of it," he said. "You seemed like you needed it more. Don't make it weird, kid."

Even after knowing Lucky for only a short time, this was something Nugget was learning about his new friend: The porcupine would complain, carp, and brag about certain things he felt he had to do for Nugget. But other things—kind things, things that showed breathtaking sensitivity—Lucky would rush over, as if he was embarrassed anyone had seen him doing them.

Case in point: "Now eat up and stay still!" Lucky snapped. "And chew with your mouth closed, or this will all have been pointless. I gotta go put on a show for my fans." Then he backed out of the log, causing the children gathered around the enclosure to cheer, with at least one yelling, "Mom! Dad! He's here! The porcupine is here!"

And so, for the first time in his or possibly any dog's life, Nugget ate his food slowly. He ate it slowly so that he could chew more quietly. He ate it slowly so that he could savor the meal, not yet knowing where his next one would come from. He ate it slowly to avoid getting quills in his teeth.

And he ate it slowly so he could watch Lucky at work. Through his narrow view out the log's front opening, Nugget watched Lucky wander back and forth across his enclosure, occasionally pushing his red rubber ball, occasionally stopping to groom his quills. The audience ate it all up. In the early going, Lucky appeared to do all these things with a permanent private eye roll (at one point, he stopped outside the log and whispered, "The price of fame, huh?"). But as the day went on and Lucky got into the groove, he appeared to become less self-conscious. He may have acted tough, but it was clear he would do anything to make a child laugh, up to and including turning around in tight circles as if chasing his tail. He did this once or twice throughout the afternoon, and each time it generated roars of delight from the families watching.

And each time, in the brief flashes when his face was in Nugget's line of sight, Nugget could have sworn he saw the porcupine smiling to himself.

Why did Lucky push people away if he loved them so much? It reminded Nugget of something, but he couldn't think of what. Reflecting on all this made Nugget feel tired, as if he'd been chasing his *own* tail. It was also warm in the sunbaked log, and presented with nothing else to do and a newly full belly (albeit one that felt kind of funny—maybe the melon had disagreed with him?), Nugget felt his head sink lower and lower, and then onto the now-familiar bark of the log, and then once more off into sleep.

When Nugget woke up, Lucky was curled up asleep next to him. The air had grown cool and still; it seemed that the visitors had all left the park, and the sun had set once more. Nugget wasn't sure if he was relieved or sad. In either case, he had something more pressing to focus on: That funny feeling in his stomach had only grown stronger.

"Lucky?" Nugget whispered. And then, slightly louder: "Lucky!"

Nothing. He would have poked Lucky to wake him up, but, well, you know. Porcupine.

Fortunately for Nugget, his stomach took care of it.

GrrruRRrumbleeEEEEeeeerrggg!!!!

Lucky opened one eye, gazing wearily at Nugget.

"I don't feel so good," Nugget said, and a second later his stomach seconded the motion: *grrworlOrrrrb!*

Lucky sighed and hauled himself to his feet.

"Yeah," he said, stretching his front and hind legs,

respectively. "I worried this might happen. Based on what I know from the informational plaques outside the wolf exhibit, I don't think canines are supposed to eat a fruit-only diet."

With that, he made his way out of the log, before turning around to look expectantly at Nugget.

"Well?" he said. "You wanted to see the zoo? Then come on, kid. We're goin' on a food drive."

17
The Tour Guide

Following Lucky through the Franklin Park Zoo that night, Nugget quickly learned two things.

One: The world was full of more animals, and *stranger* animals, than Nugget could possibly ever have imagined.

Two: Lucky knew all of them. Personally.

"Hey, Lucky!" called out a voice, its source invisible to Nugget, as they approached an enclosure ten times the size of Lucky's. "Out for a night stroll?"

"You know it!" Lucky said, looking up. Way up. Nugget followed his gaze until he saw who Lucky was speaking to: giraffes, several of them, tall as the trees and moving gracefully about the enclosure in, swaying, orange-and-brown pairs. Their horns were like antennae; their necks were like construction cranes. Nugget, who up until now had mostly sorted the world into "cute" and "not cute," had no idea where to sort the giraffes. But he knew, instantly, that he liked them. On the far side of the enclosure, a couple of baby giraffes slept soundly. Nugget wondered if they'd want to be friends with him, if somehow they ever met during the day. He hoped so.

"Who's the new kid?" the nearest giraffe asked, bending their neck downward for a better look.

"Don't even get me started," Lucky said. "He says his name's Nugget. Oh jeez, there, I've started. Hey, you guys got any meat? Or fish, or peanut butter? We're tryin' to help this kid get some good braai."

"Braai?" Nugget whispered.

"It means barbecue," Lucky said. "These guys know what I'm talkin' about, don't ya?"

The giraffes nodded, which was possibly even more exciting than seeing a porcupine nod.

"Sorry, though," the nearest giraffe said. "All we eat here is leaves and greens."

Lucky shrugged.

"Yehr, I figured. Worth a shot, though, right? Hey, go, Sox!"

Nugget followed Lucky away from the enclosure, but not before his canine hearing picked up the giraffes whispering bemusedly far above them.

"Did *you* know what a braai was?"

"Man, I don't even know who the Sox are. That porcupine is something else."

They had more luck at their next stop: the den of the muntjac deer. Nugget had never heard of muntjac deer before, but the doe who came forth to witness their arrival looked like a regular deer, with one notable exception: two streaks of dark brown fur slashed down her face, meeting on her nose in a sharp V. It reminded Nugget of the brown fur that streaked down his own nose.

"Oh, sure, we have a little meat left over," the muntjac said gently, once Lucky had done his song and dance. "I save it for if I get the midnight munchies. Here you go, dear."

"Thank you!" Nugget said, as the deer pushed her midnight snack up to the bars of her enclosure. With the effort and ingenuity so often found in hungry puppies, Nugget was able to use his long tongue to pull the food through the fence, barely chewing each bite before he swallowed it. Every mouthful settled his stomach, the new food groups helping to put right what had fallen out of balance.

Lucky made polite small talk with the muntjac about the weather and something called a "Mac Jones" while Nugget ate. When he saw that Nugget was just about finished, Lucky asked, "Alright, kid. You still hungry?"

Nugget paused, licking stray food molecules off his nose. The truth was, Nugget was always hungry, so it wasn't really a useful indicator for whether he needed more food. He probably didn't *have* to keep eating right now.

But if he said that he *did*, he would get to spend more time with Lucky exploring the zoo.

He nodded. "Yeah," he said. "I'm, like, *so* hungry."

Lucky rolled his eyes dramatically toward the muntjac. "You hear that?" he asked, pronouncing it *y'heeah*. "No good deed goes unpunished. Kid, you wouldn't happen to just be trying to use me as yer tour guide, are ya? Remember what I said about that?"

Nugget looked at the muntjac, the brown V of her face crinkling up into a wry smile. Then he looked back at Lucky and thought about what he'd seen that afternoon. Specifically, he thought about the porcupine who would do anything to make a child happy, even if he refused to admit it.

"But Mr. Lucky," Nugget said. "You're so smah—I mean, smart. I know it's *such* a bother, but I just want to learn from you."

Lucky considered this.

"I suppose being such a repository of accumulated wisdom does come with certain obligations," he said.

"I don't know what most of those words mean," Nugget said, confused.

"Exactly my point." Lucky nodded seriously. "Alright. Let's show you the ways of the world. And I mean the *entire* world."

And he did. Together, Lucky and Nugget saw red pandas from China, absurdly adorable tree climbers who looked like raccoons dipped in orange paint, and who were nocturnal just like Lucky. It turned out they were omnivorous as well and had some grains to give to Nugget. They saw a sloth from South America, but it was hard to tell if she was sleeping or just taking a very long time to respond. Outside Gorilla

Grove, they passed a peacock from Pakistan, wandering just as freely around the zoo as Lucky and Nugget. When Nugget went to say hi, the peacock's feathers flared up like a weaponized ball gown; Lucky quickly flared his own quills up in return and urged Nugget to keep walking.

"Can't trust big birds," Lucky grumbled as they hurried away from the peacock. "That's a porcupine motto. Can't trust little birds either, but at least they're not *big*."

"I didn't know that," Nugget said politely. Privately, he recalled that, as they'd left Lucky's enclosure earlier that night, he'd seen a plaque by the zookeepers' hut listing large birds as a main predator of the porcupine.

"See?" Lucky said. "This is exactly the kinda thing I need to teach you."

Whenever they came to an exhibit with particularly good leftovers, Nugget dug in, and thanked them, and Lucky implied—in an offhanded way, almost as if he couldn't even be bothered to say it—that some more food should be set aside for Nugget the next night as well.

Around the third or fourth time this happened, the words sunk in for Nugget: *the next night.*

"Wait," Nugget said. "Do you mean we'll be doing this again tomorrow?"

"Why do you always have to make it weird, kid?" Lucky asked. "Come on. The sun's coming up. Let's go home."

Home.

If Lucky heard the significance in his own words, he didn't show it. But Nugget heard it.

He loved it.

They went home.

18
The Porcupine's Dilemma

Thus began the second happy chapter of Nugget's life. By day, he would sleep, wake up, nibble on a little fruit (but not *too* much), smile at Lucky's showboating for the crowd, and go back to sleep. By night, he and Lucky would leg it out of the enclosure, wandering from one side of the zoo to the other.

Each night, the hole between the chain-link fence and the zookeepers' hut seemed to get a little smaller. After a week or two, Nugget realized that the hole was not getting smaller; he, ever the growing puppy, was in fact getting bigger. Soon it might be as tight a squeeze for him to wriggle in and out of the enclosure as it was for Lucky. Soon after that, it might even be tighter. Every night, the moment Nugget thought about any of this, he proceeded to think with great determination about absolutely anything else. But then the sun would rise, and set again, and in that time, the gap between fur and fence would grow just that much smaller.

Before long, Nugget was making all sorts of friends, and feeding on a world's worth of cuisine, so long as Lucky deemed it safe. They visited prairie dogs and tree frogs, white-bearded wildebeests and Welsh Mountain sheep. They encountered mammals, marsupials, and millipedes. Nugget loved them all—and with his positive attitude, adorable appearance, and unending eagerness to please, it wasn't long before the denizens of the Franklin Park Zoo loved him back.

The only animals they never visited were the lions. Nugget could smell meat emanating from beyond the high fences of the lions' den, in quantities so vast as to put all the other animals' lunches to shame—but the moment Nugget even looked in the den's direction, Lucky would always nudge him onward, past the den, to safety. And a nudge from a porcupine was frequently a high-stakes affair, so.

The love between Nugget and his new neighbors did not go unnoticed.

"You ever notice how everyone likes you?" Lucky asked one day.

It was probably the nicest thing Lucky had ever said to Nugget. Of course, he managed to make it sound like an accusation, but in the past few weeks, Nugget had gotten pretty good at deciphering Lucky Language.

"Everybody likes you too, y'know," Nugget said. "They get so excited when they see you coming to visit."

"*Psssh.*" Lucky fluffed out his quills, which Nugget now recognized as a clear sign he felt bashful. "They're just happy cuz they know I'm bringing you. I know these guys, yehr, but you make friends like . . . like it's *easy*. Why is that?"

"Is it not easy for you to make friends?" Nugget asked.

His surprise was genuine, but so was Lucky's stony silence. Clearly, Nugget had hit a nerve.

"Well," Nugget said, "I don't know. Everyone is so nice here, so that helps. But also ever since I was young—"

"You're still young, kid."

"Well, ever since I was *younger* . . . I'm . . . I mean, people have *told* me that—I mean, a lot of people *seem* to think that . . ."

"Eish, my bru, just spit it out, we'll be here till sunrise."

"That I'm cute," Nugget said, feeling instantly foolish.

Lucky continued to say nothing. They were lying in the log after a long and enjoyable night of nibbling on red panda snacks, but as Nugget's words hung in the air, he flashed back to another time and place entirely, one he had tried never to flash back to—the last night he had seen his mother.

"I know. I know," he said hurriedly, Wendy's words coming back to him unbidden. "You're going to say 'I hope you don't think your cuteness is what gives you value. What gives you value is the way you love.'"

"What?" Lucky snorted. "No. Are you kidding? Your cuteness is your entire value."

Nugget did not expect this.

"I mean, don't get me wrong," Lucky quickly added. "You're a nice kid, kid. Y'know. If you're into that sort of thing."

"Into . . . being nice?"

"Right. Exactly. But let me tell you: Not everyone is. Which is why it's so important to have something else. Anything else. A gimmick. An edge. Something to make people like you. Mine is to be silly, someone the kids can laugh at, so they don't just see me as a threat. Yours is to be wicked cute."

Nugget thought about Lucky, turning in circles for children all day.

"Lucky," he said, "I don't think those kids are laughing *at* you. They're laughing *with* you. They think you're cute too. Didn't you ever think people might just like you for you?"

"I could ask you the same question," Lucky snapped back, and while Nugget was used to the porcupine pretending to be grumpy, these words had real bite. Lucky must have felt Nugget's surprise, because his next words came swiftly and much more softly.

"Kid," he said. "Have you ever heard of the porcupine's dilemma?"

Nugget wracked his brain. Lucky was always complaining that the zookeepers should be giving him a quarterly bonus melon, but somehow Nugget guessed this wasn't that.

"Say you have a couple porcupines out in the cold at night," Lucky said. "Maybe they want to huddle up together for warmth. Maybe they want to huddle up for safety. Maybe one of them just wants a hug. But no matter how bad they want it . . . they can't do it. Too many spiky bits in the way.

The closer they get to anyone, the more everyone's going to get hurt. The way I see it, that's life. You can't rely too much on anyone else. You can't get your hopes up for someone to like you. It only ends in pain."

"But you don't actually *have* to worry about that," Nugget said. "I mean, I live in a log with you, and I've only gotten poked twice. Okay, three times."

"That's not what I . . . Kid, do you know what a metaphor is?"

Nugget frowned. "Is that like a marsupial?"

Lucky sighed.

"Look," he said. "I came here from overseas, right? Even if I *wanted* to test out the porcupine's dilemma, I couldn't. I'm the only porcupine I know. I'm a danger to the rest of you here who don't have any spiky bits at all. You saw it yourself, as soon as you met me—you leaped away like I was a monster."

Guilt pierced through Nugget like a stray quill. He *had* thought Lucky was a monster.

But now he knew better. He banished his guilty thoughts and focused on the thoughts that would help.

"I didn't know who you were then," he said. "But you chose to let me stay with you anyway. That makes you the opposite of a monster. Someone told me once that family is whoever you choose who also chooses you back. So what if I can't hug you? I can still choose you. Anyone who knows you would."

There was silence once more in the log. But this time it didn't smell of stress or resentment.

It smelled of surprise. And of unspoken, unspeakable gratitude.

"Like I said, kid," Lucky said at last. "You're nice."

In Lucky Language, that *was* a hug.

"You're nice too." Nugget smiled.

"Don't make it weird, kid. Good night."

Lucky rolled over and, after a span of time so short that no living being could possibly have fallen asleep within it, set about fake snoring loudly.

As fake snores gradually turned into real snores, Nugget was lulled to sleep himself. He slept long and hard, smiling through dreams of a world in which porcupines and puppies were able to hug safely.

When he woke up, it was the middle of the night again, and Lucky was nowhere to be found. Nugget's dreams had been so sweet, he must have slept through the entire day, and then slept through his usual post-sunset breakfast time to boot. Indeed, as he poked his head out of the log, he saw Lucky pushing his way back into the enclosure, having already been out for a nighttime walk.

Nugget smiled, waiting for Lucky to make a wisecrack about how lazy Nugget was and how kids these days were sleeping their lives away.

As soon as Lucky did not take the easy chance to gripe at Nugget, Nugget knew something was terribly wrong.

"We have a problem," Lucky said, his voice deadly serious. "They know."

"What?" Nugget asked. "Know what? Who's *they*?"

But he knew the answer, knew it before Lucky even spat out the words.

"The zookeepers," Lucky said. "They're onto us. They've fortified the fences. There's no more extra food. They're smoking you out."

"Okay," Nugget said, even though this wasn't okay at all. "I'll go somewhere. I'll go back to the bear cages. I'll—"

"No." Lucky cut him short. "You're not going anywhere. I am."

"Where?"

There was determination in Lucky's scrunching eyes. Determination and the sadness of a porcupine who had just managed to huddle up close to someone.

"That's easy," he said. "I'm going into the lions' den."

19

The Lions' Den

"We really don't have to do this," Nugget said, chasing Lucky down the darkened promenade of the Franklin Park Zoo. Well, Nugget could still run much faster than Lucky—even faster, actually, now that he'd grown some more—so he wasn't so much *chasing* the porcupine as he was circling around him repeatedly. But that was the thing about a determined porcupine: Unless you had thought to bring body armor, you really couldn't stop one from getting where it wanted to go.

"You're right," Lucky said, not slowing down. "*We* don't have to do this. *I* do. I have spikes. You don't. I know these animals. You don't. I'll go in, get the extra meat—because you just *know* the zookeepers wouldn't dare to cut down on those fat cats' food—and bring it back to you. Just another day in the life of Lucky, the most put-upon, selfless animal guardian on two continents."

The return of Lucky's ability to kvetch was a relief to Nugget, but only a mild one, as the porcupine kept plowing forward. Soon they would reach their terrible destination.

The lions' den was at the very top of a steep slope, above

the slow-moving camels, above the red river hog, as if the zoo-keepers had known that the king of the jungle would want to be put at the peak of the animal pyramid. After making your way up the winding path, you found yourself at the edge of a craggy cliff, the rock face of the hill suddenly dropping down dozens of feet—and then swooping back up away from you in a man-made canyon.

The canyon had been put there to protect you. So had the waterfall and ensuing river that ran through it. So had the two giant plates of thick glass on either side of the canyon, and the fence directly in front of the canyon, a fence no human could climb.

But Lucky was no human.

"Think about this for a second!" Nugget pleaded as Lucky hooked his claws into the fence chain, pulling himself upward like it was just another tree on the savanna.

"This isn't worth putting yourself in danger for," Nugget continued. "We don't know how much longer I can fit in the log with you anyway. I'm getting bigger. Maybe this is a sign it's time to stop hiding! Maybe if we let the zookeepers find out about me, they'll let me stay!

"That's your problem, kid," Lucky said, already halfway up the fence. "You trust people too much."

"I don't!" Nugget cried. "I *really* don't! I didn't know if I'd ever trust anyone again until I met you! That's why I don't want to lose you!"

Lucky turned at the top of the fence, looking down at Nugget. His eyes were unreadable. He smelled like every emotion at once.

"Face it, kid," he said. "You're stuck with me."

Nugget thought about a few things.

He thought about how sad he'd felt after being alone for even just a day or two, and how Lucky had been alone much, much longer than that.

He thought about the porcupine's dilemma, and how scary it must have been for Lucky to let himself get this close to someone.

And he thought about what his mother had once told him, about the ways people showed you they loved you. It wasn't always just by saying the words. Sometimes it was by doing something infuriating, something scary, something they felt they had to do because they wanted the best for you.

"Okay," Nugget said. "Go. But I'll be waiting right here the entire time. And be *safe*!"

"Of *course* I'll be safe," Lucky said. "Those lazy house cats are going to sleep through the whole thing. You think I'm risking my hide for *you*, kid? Eish, grow up."

Of course, he was risking more than just his hide. But rather than argue the point further, Nugget just sat and watched, heart beating out of his chest, as Lucky turned back to face the other side of the fence.

And dropped over it.

With surprising grace, Lucky landed on a ledge so small and precarious, it barely qualified as a ledge. As the porcupine began picking his way nimbly down the side of the cliff, Nugget realized that he'd watched his friend waddle around the ground for weeks now, but never actually seen him in a true South African–style environment with all its mountains, trees, and troughs. Here, Lucky was at home. In no time at all, he had made his way to the ground, where he floated across the river with the help of his hollow quills. Once across, he shook himself out and began climbing his way back up the other side of the canyon. As soon as he reached the top, he turned to look back across the gap. At first, Nugget assumed he was going to brag. But when Lucky wiggled his nose impatiently, Nugget understood: He was waiting for directions.

Nugget closed his eyes and sniffed. The meat smell was coming from just a few yards past where Lucky was now, floating up from behind a rocky outcropping. Nugget opened his eyes and nodded his head in the direction of the rocks, and Lucky nodded back, turned, and shuffled off in that direction, staying low to the ground all the while.

When he came to the rocky outcropping, he disappeared behind it for a second.

Then ten seconds.

Then thirty.

The entire time, Nugget held his breath.

It wasn't until the moment Lucky reappeared, holding a

steak triumphantly in his mouth and dragging it along the ground behind him, that Nugget allowed himself to believe that this was going to work.

And it wasn't until the moment after that Nugget saw it: From way in the shadowy back of the enclosure, a shape had just moved in the darkness. Like desert dust kicked into the air, the movement loosened a smell that was rusty, and primordial, and *hungry*.

One of the lions was awake.

And now it was stalking straight toward Lucky.

20
Love

Lucky continued ambling toward the front edge of the enclosure, clueless as to what was coming, his senses presumably flooded with steak and pride. Nugget's first instinct was to bark, to whine, to make any sort of noise that would alert Lucky to the danger he was in. Nugget had only seen *one* shape move in the darkness—which meant any number of other lions might be sleeping somewhere just out of view. Barking would wake them, and waking them would take the current situation from crisis to nightmare.

But there was already a nightmare quality to the way Nugget could see Lucky's every move, could see him stop to pull the steak over a sticky clump of weeds, and all Nugget could do was sit in silence and watch in horror from beyond the fence.

The fence.

It was made to keep children safe from lions and lions safe from themselves. Nugget was bigger than he once had been, but not so big that anyone might rationally have expected him to be able to clear the barrier in front of him.

But if you have ever come home from a day out of the house and found your counters empty, your floors messy, your walls scratched, and somehow, bafflingly, your hung-up laundry covered in fur, you will know: There is nothing rational about what a puppy can achieve when it loves you and wants to be near you.

Before his mind had time to think about it, Nugget's body had backed away down the hill—and then come dashing back, like a slingshot released, reaching blurring speed in a manner of moments. After careening up the lumpy fake rock encasing the lions' den's viewing glass, Nugget bounced like a self-propelled pinball off the side of the rocks and over the top of the fence, his front paws catching on the edge just long enough for his back paws to meet and then *push*, sending him flying, front paws outstretched, across the narrow canyon. He landed, just barely, on the far side, hitting the ground with a force that knocked the wind out of him. He tumbled over himself like a poorly skipped stone, bouncing across the enclosure until he should have by all means been down for the count.

But Nugget would not stay down. Immediately he leaped to his feet, finding himself face-to-face with a stunned Lucky, whose mouth had dropped open in surprise, causing the steak to drop with it.

"Have you lost yer *mahbles*?!" Lucky squealed.

"You have to go," Nugget whispered. "Run. Now. I'll buy you time. I'm smaller and faster than you, so you need more time than I do. So go. Now. *Please.*"

"What in the world are you—"

And then Nugget heard it: the long, low growl.

This time, it wasn't from Nugget's stomach.

Slowly, as if delaying the sight could make it less real, Lucky turned around. Once fully rotated, he joined Nugget in staring in horror as, out of the shadows, a shape emerged. It was a shape designed for stalking whomever it wanted to, for stopping whenever it wanted to, for not having to move too fast because it was simply never necessary—until, of course, it wanted to.

The lion locked eyes on both of them. She tilted her head curiously, looking from porcupine to puppy and back again.

She seemed to be deciding what to do next. She didn't typically come across this type of meat—let alone meat that moved.

"Go," Nugget whispered.

"*You* go!" Lucky hissed. "*I'm* the one with the quills, remember? Cats all up and down Africa know not to mess with me!"

It was the way the lion's head kept tilting from one side to the other that made Nugget ask the next question.

"Do you think this lion grew up in Africa?" he whispered. "Or do you think maybe she doesn't know not to mess with you?"

For once, Lucky had nothing to say, no biting comeback.

The only response he gave was a burst of scent: the nostril-clogging smell of sudden, pure, acrid fear.

"Go," Nugget repeated. "I'll be right after you. Quick, before she makes a move! Go!"

"No!" Lucky spat. "You're under my care, kid! That makes you my—my—"

"I know," Nugget said.

He turned away from the lion just long enough to look Lucky in the eyes.

"I love you too," Nugget said.

And then he nipped the porcupine on his big, honking nose.

Lucky squealed in surprise and pain, backing up instinctively, putting him that much farther away than Nugget from the lion.

The lion darted forward. Nugget turned and barked, and from pure confusion, the lion froze in her tracks, one paw outstretched, her heavy and hurt-tipped claws hanging in the air. Who *dared*? she seemed to wonder. *What* dared? What was this *thing* doing in her domain?

Hopefully making a quick retreat, Nugget thought, and turned around long enough to see that Lucky was indeed waddling as fast as his little legs could carry him toward the canyon. Nugget ran after him, around him, barking up a storm, growling any time the confused lion came near, shepherding the best friend he had in the world closer to safety. More

97

than a friend. The person who had taken him in when all had seemed lost, who had taught Lucky something about what it meant to have character. To have a home. To have family.

To love.

By now, Nugget's barking had drawn another shape from the darkness: a male lion, shaking the sleep out of his great mane, clearly unhappy about having been woken up. He growled in complaint, and hearing this, the lioness decided to bring things to a close. That was fine by Nugget. They were almost out. If they could just get Lucky a little—closer—to—the canyon—

They were inches away from the edge of the enclosure when the lioness suddenly swiped her paw toward them, her killing claws out and on display.

Looking back on it later, it was Nugget's love for Lucky above all else that gave him the courage to leap one more time into the air, throwing himself into the narrow space between Lucky and lion, flying over the cliff-hanging edge between safety and nothing at all.

Because Nugget's love had indeed finally given him unimaginable strength.

And so it was also Nugget's love—along with a lion's claws—that finally tore him apart.

Part Two

UGLY

21
Dog Dreams

Dogs dream.

The signs, if you have ever seen them, are unmistakable. Their legs twitch in their sleep. The tail lifts and thumps back down with a sluggish thud as if wagging through molasses. The muzzle quivers as the dreamer makes a soft, repeated sound that nine out of ten canine sleep scientists have gone on the record describing as *a-bloop-bloop-bloop-bloop-bloop*.

It is the sound of imagination unleashed. It is the sound of a squirrel being chased in another dimension.

It is a sound you may already know well.

Something you may *not* know is that, for whatever reason, small dogs have more dreams and move through them more quickly than their larger canine counterparts. Big dogs have dreams that last as long as five minutes at a time (though for the dog who is dreaming, they may seem to last for hours or even years). Small dogs, meanwhile, are thought to cycle through dreams at rapid sixty-second intervals, running through a multitude of new worlds every night before they wake up again. In short: Puppies' heads are full of dreams.

This is, for the record, not artistic license. This is a real scientific fact about dogs that you can look up.

(Of course, everything else in this story is also a real scientific fact, including the talking porcupines. Those bits are just harder to find online.)

Anyway. Back to the point.

Nugget had had many short dreams in his short life. Dreams of playing fetch with his mother. Dreams about bears dancing under the moonlight. Dreams where Mrs. Vandyck decided Nugget and his siblings could have all the human food they'd ever wanted, plus some extra to share with Lucky, the red pandas, and the baby giraffes.

But he'd never had a dream like the one he was having right now.

"Thankfully, his condition is stable. No new bleeding, except internally."

"The internal bleeding is what I'm worried about."

"We need to do a lot of things. One emergency at a time here. I've never seen a situation this . . . ugly."

Emergency. Bleeding. Ugly. The words should have set off alarm bells in Nugget's head, but it was hard to be alarmed about anything right now. For one thing, this was obviously a dream. He'd never been in a room this clean before, this spotless and white and cool, except for when the Vandycks had taken him to Dr. Sheynberg's veterinary office. And no visit to the veterinarian had ever involved four people in face masks and scrubs, all staring down at Nugget from above.

So this was a dream.

So there was no emergency.

"They didn't find *any* identification on him? A collar? A chip?"

"None. He must have been a stray. They just found him this morning, first thing, on their morning rounds, near the water. You know the strangest thing?"

"Scalpel. What?"

"Well, the guy who dropped him off said the reason they looked in the water at all was because there was a porcupine outside the exhibit. Said it was squeaking its little head off. It had gone crazy and gotten out of its own enclosure."

"Look, can we quit gossiping about porcupines? A life is at stake here. Gauze!"

Oh, this was a *good* dream. In this dream, Lucky had made it out of the lion exhibit! He was safe! Nugget had saved him. He couldn't wait to tell him all about it when he woke up.

Nugget didn't think to question how he could know Lucky was safe in the real world, if this was only a dream.

That was dream logic for you.

"Hold on. Did his tail just move? Is it *wagging*?"

"Whoa. His heart rate is rising. Up the anesthesia."

"Will do. Poor little guy. He wouldn't be wagging his tail if he knew . . ."

Nugget was vaguely interested in hearing the end of that sentence, but suddenly, his brain was flooded with chemicals reminding him: Who cares? You're asleep. Sleeping is *great*. You should really focus on sleeping right now.

Anyway, this had to be a dream. Because there was one other thing that had been going on the whole time that was simply, utterly impossible.

The last time Nugget remembered being awake, the whole world had smelled like blood, and bone, and running water.

Wherever he was now, the world smelled like . . . nothing at all.

And for a dog? That was impossible.

So Nugget fell back into dreams.

22

Gimme Shelter

Nugget woke up.

This was not a dream.

Dreams weren't this painful, for one thing. He must have sprained something in his wild rush to save Lucky, because his front right paw throbbed with a dull ache. And the ground was too cold. After weeks of sleeping on grassy, needled bark, the cool man-made tile came as a tangible surprise, like cold water thrown over the brain.

He stood up gingerly, keeping his weight off his hurt paw. He was in a kennel-sized pen, the door made of thin metal bars allowing him to see out into a hallway. Across that hallway were more kennels, just like Nugget's, each one containing a dog not at *all* just like Nugget. One was a big, dozing pit bull; another was a small Chihuahua, pacing back and forth; a third was something large, curly, and presumably ending in *-oodle*, yipping and yelping for no apparent reason.

Well, there was one possible reason the doodle might be yipping: to fit in. The air was alive with barking, whining, meowing, and hissing. If Nugget strained his ears enough to filter through the noise, he could even hear the occasional *caw* of birds.

(He still couldn't smell anything, though. Why couldn't he smell anything?)

For any other dog, this may have been stressful. Nugget, though, just smiled.

(Smiling hurt. Why did *smiling* hurt?)

"Hey!" he said through the bars.

The yapping doodle stopped yapping. The pacing Chihuahua stopped pacing. Both of them stared at Nugget but did not speak. Weird.

The dozing pit bull, meanwhile, opened one eye.

"What's up?" asked the pit bull, neglecting to lift his head, or even open his other eye. "Are you, uh . . . okay?"

"Yeah, I'm fine," Nugget said. The pit bull didn't seem convinced, but Nugget was telling the truth. "Don't worry," he continued, to prove it. "I've actually been living here in the zoo for a while now. I was just wondering . . . what exhibit, exactly, is this? I don't think I knew about this one."

Apparently, this surprised the pit bull enough to warrant opening both eyes.

"Zoo?" he said. "This ain't no zoo. I mean, I don't know what a zoo is, but this probably ain't it. Hey, are you sure you're okay?"

"Yeah, of course," Nugget said, confused. "Why?"

"Okay. Phew." The pit bull began to close his eyes again.

"Wait!" Nugget cried. "What, uh . . . what's your name?"

"Huh." The pit bull paused. "Okay, you got me. That's a good question."

Before Nugget could ask what in the world that meant, the pit bull rose, stretched, yawned, and padded lazily forward. Nugget's heart panged as he was reminded of Lucky's unhurried waddle. For reasons Nugget could not quite name at this time, he knew Lucky was safe, but he still urgently wanted to find him and learn what had happened. He just had to figure out what part of the zoo he was in first. And why the animals here acted so oddly.

At the front of the pen, the pit bull angled his head as far to the right as he could. A small tag dangled from his collar, bouncing off the bars of his pen door with a soft *ting*.

"Hey, Sparky," he said.

Sparky was either the Chihuahua's name or just a description she responded to, because she now darted forward to her own pen door, where she popped her head right out through the bars, her large ears flattening against them and then flapping back out again.

"What's up?" Sparky asked, turning left to look at the pit bull.

"What's my name this time?" the pit bull asked.

"Maurice," the Chihuahua said. "That's what they've been calling you."

"Thanks, Sparky."

"No problem, Maurice."

Sparky's ears briefly folded over her eyes as she pulled herself back into her kennel. Then she began pacing again, as if it were very important she do so. For some reason, she seemed to be avoiding looking at Nugget. Maurice, however, turned back to face him.

"I'm Maurice," said Maurice.

"You didn't know your own *name?*" Nugget felt he had missed several crucial updates somewhere.

"Never got one," Maurice shrugged. "Not one that stuck anyway."

"In here, if you don't come in with a collar, you don't come in with a name," said Sparky. She still wasn't looking at Nugget (why wasn't she looking at Nugget?), but she did at least seem willing to acknowledge him now. "So they make one up and give it to you. Why, you got one already?"

"Nugget," said Nugget.

"Cool. Good luck telling 'em that," the pit bull said, not unsympathetically.

"Telling who? Who's 'em? I mean, them? I mean—hold on—who are *they?*"

"The workers here," Sparky said. "Look, Maurice doesn't know what a zoo is, but I do. So. Imagine if there were a zoo with way fewer outside parts and fewer visitors and just for pets. *Not* to be confused with a petting zoo."

"Hold on," Nugget said. "You mean I'm *not* still in the Franklin Park Zoo?"

"Franklin Park? Oh, man."

Finally, Sparky turned and looked Nugget in the eyes. Upon seeing her expression, Nugget kind of wished she hadn't.

"We're miles away from Franklin Park," Sparky said. "You're in Father Patrick's Last Chance Animal Shelter."

23

On Second Thought, Maybe Do Not Gimme Shelter

Oh no. How was Nugget going to get to Lucky now? And what was it Mrs. Vandyck had said, pleading with Taylor over the dinner table? *We certainly don't want to send them to some over-burdened animal shelter.* At the time, he'd had no idea what an "animal shelter" was, but now he was locked up in one, and judging by the sheer number of opinionated animals he heard around him, it was pretty overburdened already.

As if on cue, the doodle let loose with another round of barking, prompting a chorus of agitated pet sounds from all around the shelter.

"Hey, hey, hey!" Sparky yelled over the din. "Let's all calm down, okay? There're way worse places to be than here. For one thing, this is a live-release shelter. That means even if no one adopts you, you're going to be fine. That's why we call it the Last Chance: because they really do give you the last chance you'll ever need. Trust me. Some places don't give you that chance at all."

"Yeah, and they feed us here and take care of us and let us play every day. And you never know when you're gonna get adopted!" Maurice chimed in. "Like, the visitors are coming soon, and most of them are here to take us to their homes. I've already been in three!"

"Wait," Nugget said. "Adopted?"

"Yeah! Of course, it helps if you're small and cute. I'm not that small, but I think people like my big head. I've been told it's 'remarkably square.'" The pit bull beamed with pride.

"Yeah, I've been meaning to ask about that," Sparky said. "You're such a sweetheart. Why do you keep getting returned?"

"Couches," Maurice said ruefully. "They're so delicious."

No wonder all the dogs here were so nervous. On that day when Nugget and his siblings had been up for adoption, he had been shocked and confused at the idea that you could love a new family as much as you loved your first one.

Now, in the wake of his time at the Franklin Park Zoo, he knew that it was possible to make all sorts of new friends. Maybe this wouldn't be so bad.

And cute? Nugget's *breed* was cute!

Despite himself, he smiled wide.

Okay, that *really* hurt. And Sparky had *definitely* winced when Nugget did it.

In fact: "Maurice, don't tell him this stuff," she was saying. "You'll just get his hopes up."

"Why shouldn't he tell me that?" Nugget asked. "And
why won't you look at me for more than two seconds? Also, why
doesn't it *smell* like anything here?"

"Wait," said Sparky. "Do you not know?"

"Know *what*?" Nugget asked.

Just then, the world exploded in sound. A door at the end of
the hallway had been opened, and all the woofing and whining
and squawking that had just begun to die down suddenly rose
back into a wild crescendo.

"It's visitor time!" called out a cheery voice. This, along
with the sound of footsteps, heralded the arrival of a young
woman in a baseball cap and a gray polo shirt that read
VOLUNTEER.

"Visitor time!" Maurice cried, jumping up and down on
squat legs. "My first visitor time as Maurice!"

Nugget could feel the situation getting away from him.

"Wait. What don't I know?" he asked Sparky, shouting to make himself heard over all the excitement. "What's
going on?"

Sparky looked like she was just on the verge of answer-
ing when the volunteer in the baseball cap knelt in front of
Nugget's pen.

"Hey, little guy," she said. "How're you feeling? Did you
sleep okay? You spent quite a lot of time in the clinic yesterday.

You ready to go back in for a checkup? Don't worry, you won't have to walk on that paw."

The clinic?

The *dream*.

Of course. It all made sense now. Nugget must have injured his paw while he was rescuing Lucky, and the shelter workers had done something to help patch him up. That was what he had seen last night. Something they gave him must have put him in a deep sleep, making him think he was dreaming, and the pain he felt now was due to those drugs wearing off.

The volunteer opened the door to Nugget's pen and lifted him up off the ground. Rather than wiggle or fight, Nugget just snuggled happily into the volunteer's soft polo shirt. Considering all he had been through, he felt lucky to have gotten away with just a few aches and pains. And then, on top of that, to have found these humans who wanted to help him feel even better? Things were looking up.

"Hey," Sparky said as the volunteer carried Nugget past her kennel. Her tone was strangely somber. "The clinic has a mirror. When you're in there . . . you're going to want to look in it."

"Great! Thanks for the tip!" Nugget chirped over the volunteer's shoulder as he was led away down the hall.

Sparky didn't reply.

The volunteer carried Nugget down the hallway and out

into a lobby full of human families, all waiting for visiting hours to begin. Nugget smiled at the children as he passed. This was his first chance to make a good impression, and he intended to put it to good use. He didn't mean to brag, but Lucky himself had pointed it out: First impressions were sort of Nugget's thing. It came with being cute. The only exception he'd ever encountered was that lion, and honestly Nugget wasn't convinced that they couldn't have found a way to be friends, if only they'd been given more time to learn what they had in common.

That said . . .

For some reason, the children in the lobby gasped when Nugget passed. Some looked away from him just like Sparky had. One baby even looked up, saw Nugget, and buried its face in its parent's shoulder.

And the parents, somehow, were less well behaved than the kids: They recoiled, couldn't look, or looked too long.

And on top of this, Nugget still couldn't smell anything.

Don't worry, Nugget told himself, even though he was starting to do just that. *There's really no point in worrying about what's going on.* In a moment, he could simply look in the mirror and find out.

Then they were across the lobby and entering a cool, clean, all-white room: the clinic.

There, the volunteer pulled Nugget gently from her shoulder and placed him on an elevated table.

The last time Nugget had been here, he'd been too woozy with pain and pain medicine to take in his surroundings. Now he was alert, awake, and able to turn and see his reflection.

So he did.

Nugget turned.

He looked in the mirror.

And he found out.

24
How Nugget Looked Now

Nugget's face was gone.

Well, mostly. The big brown eyes were still there. So was one of the big, floppy ears, the one on the right. But everything else . . .

The other ear, to start. It had been torn in two. What remained of Nugget's left ear was gouged and scored, the cuts running like dried-up riverbeds through fur.

The fur. Whole patches of his coat were missing, from the top of Nugget's head, to much of his right flank, to the very tip of his tail. The bald patch on his torso bore the red X of a double-slashed scar.

The scars. There was the X, of course, and the tears on the right ear. But one scar in particular ran diagonal down Nugget's face, like a paltry unfinished half imitation of the muntjac deer's brown V. But instead of that smooth, rich brown, the facial scar seemed to shift color to become whatever was most offensive to the fur it was passing through at any given point. It seared livid scarlet through Nugget's white fur, clashed like muddy rust with a stripe of black fur, and ended, oozing purple, upon reaching his rich brown snout, before the whole wicked bullet train of the scar could finish the journey through what should have been smooth, brown fur, to what should have been a round, wet nose.

Because the nose had . . .

Well.

The nose.

It had been ripped clean off.

The small, sad mercy was that the whole snout had not been removed; had that been the case, Nugget may never have survived the night. But what remained of the snout had been crumpled and cratered, and it came to an abrupt halt a half inch short of where every dog's most valuable instrument should have been.

What was there now instead looked like a strawberry gone to rot. It wasn't just an absence; it was an implosion at the tip of the face, a first impression turned foul. Underneath it, Nugget's teeth stuck up and out at odd angles, with no upper lip to hide them. Even his tongue lolled out to the side, no longer having as much space to sit in. How had he not *noticed* that? How had he not *felt* it?

But suddenly, Nugget knew: He hadn't felt it because he had not wanted to feel it. He may have wondered why he could not smell, but he had not truly wanted to know. Now, though, he knew, and there was no going back, no returning to who he had been before.

For the lion's claws had not merely injured Nugget's paw. They had made Nugget unrecognizable to himself.

Hold on, you may be thinking. *What about the difference between how someone* looks *and how they* appear? *Nugget may have thought he* looked *ugly, but couldn't he still* appear *to be all those great things he'd been before? Inquisitive, eager, animated? Aren't those all worth mentioning?*

And you would do well to keep thinking things like that as you grow older and go through life. So, you know. Good for you.

But Nugget did not know those things right now. Or if he did, he had forgotten them just as soon as he had seen his new face in the mirror. He forgot everything he liked about himself and all the things people liked about him that had nothing to do with his appearance: his curiosity, his excitement, his hope. In that moment, Nugget forgot how hope felt altogether.

All that he remembered now was a voice, the voice of someone he had trusted with his life though that life was now in the past: *Your cuteness is your entire value.*

Then another voice, one he had assumed was from a dream, but which was, in fact, his new reality:

I've never seen a situation this . . .

Ugly.

25
Hope

An animal shelter is not a good place to feel hopeless.

Hope is what binds an animal shelter together and makes it work. Hope got the residents of Father Patrick's up every morning—the hope that this was the day they might meet a loving family. And those families were drawn there by the flip side of that same hope—the hope of finding a pet as excited to meet them as they were to meet it.

Hope was even what had brought the volunteer there that morning, and every volunteer like her. It was the reason she was here helping with this poor injured dog she had heard about, who had been brave enough to go into a lions' den, and who surely deserved to feel better soon. Hope was the reason she carefully cleaned each scar on the young dog's body, making sure there was no risk of infection, applying antiseptic tenderness to this puppy's rough past in the hope of giving him a much brighter future.

And hope was why the volunteer took Nugget's complete silence and stillness throughout all this as a good sign.

Perhaps, she hoped, he was already adjusting to his new life and doing so with remarkable calm and serenity.

She was still hoping this as she carefully lifted Nugget back up out of the clinic and returned him to his kennel to join the other dogs in being considered by that day's visitors.

Not all hopes are as well founded as others.

Because if Nugget was calm, it was only the calm of someone in a self-induced coma who has decided that feeling nothing is better than feeling every bad feeling at once. If Nugget was serene, it was only the serenity of an iceberg's tip, floating just above the surface of something dark and cold and impossible to confront head-on.

This became clearer and clearer as the day went on and more children passed Nugget's pen. Where once he had leaped up to play with every child, now Nugget shied away. Once, getting noticed was all he wanted. Now being noticed hurt. Because Nugget's eyes had been left uninjured, he could see all too well how children flinched when they saw him, how adults hurried their kids on to the next pen.

That was fine by Nugget. All he wanted was for no one to look at him.

The visiting day ended. The dogs were let out into small dog runs to play and burn off energy, but Nugget, recovering as he was from surgery, was separated from the others by a thin wire gate. It was the most dogs Nugget had seen playing together since he'd lived in a comfy puppy cage with his siblings. Back then, they had tossed and tumbled over one another, and Nugget had been right in the middle of it all. Now he kept his distance from the gate, and the dogs on the other side kept theirs in turn.

At the end of playtime, the dogs returned to their pens, where they found full bowls of water and food. Nugget ate his dinner, but the loss of his sense of smell had affected his sense of taste too. What he was eating didn't taste like dog food so much as it tasted like the *idea* of dog food, being talked about in another room, in a low voice.

That was day one.

Then it was day two. Then day three. Then more.

Each day felt the same as the last. In actuality, a few changes did occur: Nugget's paw healed. His fur began to grow back. Slowly, very slowly, Nugget regained the ability to catch the faintest whiffs of scents. Sparky, perhaps feeling guilty about how she had acted on Nugget's first day, asked Nugget how he was doing each morning. Maurice was adopted. When Nugget failed to ever answer Sparky, Sparky eventually stopped asking, and then was fostered out. Maurice was returned, this time wearing a collar labeled DORIS.

But to Nugget, it all may just as well have never happened.

All Nugget had ever hoped for was to love and be loved in return. Now, though, he did not love himself, and so he could not imagine anyone else loving him. And so he felt hopeless.

But.

Hopeless is something you *feel*, not something you *are*. Even if you cannot summon a shred of hope from within yourself, it is worth sticking around because hope can walk in from outside, infusing your life with something vital when you thought all was lost. Like rain in a desert. Or hot sauce on a mediocre burrito.

In exactly this way, hope arrived for Nugget when he least expected it.

Hope was a small, tired-looking, but nevertheless kind-eyed woman in a puffy green vest.

Hope's name was Linh Trần.

26
Linh Trần

In addition to the puffy green vest, Linh Trần wore comfortable-looking tennis shoes, a rumpled blue shirt with stains all over it, and jeans exactly as dark as you would want them to be if you were likely to be getting stains all over those too. Her dark hair was pulled back in a ponytail. There were bags under her eyes and lines around her mouth when she smiled. But that was the thing: She was smiling.

And she was smiling right at Nugget.

"That one," she said.

"Are you sure, Ms. Trần?" the volunteer asked. This was not the same volunteer who had tended to Nugget's wounds on his first day in the shelter. This volunteer had come later, and had only ever known Nugget to be sullen, withdrawn, and as repelled by the shelter's visitors as they frequently were by him.

"Please. Call me Linh. And yes, I am sure."

The volunteer made one last attempt at giving all parties involved an escape clause. "It's just, normally, we ask people to take twenty-four hours to go home, think, and decide. Adopting a dog is a big decision, and we want you to be one hundred percent certain you're able to give this dog the loving home it needs to—"

"I am certain now," said Ms. Trần.

A week or two ago, this may have stirred the embers of love in Nugget's eager heart: Who was this woman? What had drawn her so quickly to him?

Now, like the volunteer, Nugget was just confused: Who *was* this woman? What had drawn her to *him*?

But it didn't matter. She had just read through a series of forms on a tablet and signed them all. Now she smiled her tired smile as the volunteer opened the door to Nugget's pen.

"Way to go, Nugget!" Doris cheered, as the volunteer led a stunned Nugget out into the hall.

Nugget was going home with someone.

Not home, said some battle-scarred part of Nugget's heart. *Just* . . . somewhere. *You are going* somewhere *with someone*.

But as Nugget was led out of the building and placed in a crate in the passenger seat of Linh Trần's car, something happened.

It was true that Nugget's ability to smell and taste had just begun to return. Unfortunately, in the shelter, there was only one thing to taste: bland, economy-priced dog food. And there were only a few things to smell: wet fur usually, impatience, and (in occasional moments that made Nugget feel like, actu-ally, smelling might be overrated) *cats*.

Linh Trần's car did not smell like any of those things.

But it did smell faintly like *something*. And given how poorly Nugget could smell right now, this meant that to a healthy nose, or even a *human* nose, the car must have been positively bursting with that smell, saturated with it like a big flower saturated with pollen.

So . . . what smell was it?

Nugget sniffed, trying to get a handle on it, but this pro-cess was hindered by the fact that, well, Nugget had more or less nothing to sniff with.

Nevertheless, Ms. Trần saw him trying to catch the new scent.

And once again, she smiled.

"You like that?" she said. "I just came back from catering a luncheon. Hold on. There's some leftovers in the back seat."

If one thing was familiar to Nugget in this strange new moment, it was *leftovers*.

He didn't dare wag his tail. He just froze as Ms. Trần vanished from sight.

As Nugget waited, suspended in time, something occurred to him: For the first time in weeks, he wanted something. He *hoped* for something.

Ms. Trần returned, holding a glistening piece of meat,

damp with the broth it had just been plucked from, and flecked with bits of green.

"Here," she said. "Try. It's got cilantro. Cilantro's good for dogs. I checked."

Nervously, Nugget moved forward, opened his lopsided mouth, and took a bite.

Immediately, his mouth was flooded with the strongest taste he'd experienced in weeks. It was the taste of hope becoming reality.

It tasted like cilantro.

Nugget chewed.

He swallowed.

And.

Look.

We all know where this is going.

Nugget fell in love again.

27
Emily Trần

A car ride is a great way to get to know someone you have just met and/or fallen in love with. Especially if that someone can carry a conversation.

Linh Trần could absolutely carry a conversation.

"My daughter is going to be so excited," she said, turning smoothly into a rotary intersection. "Emily's been asking for a dog for so long, and today while I was packing up after the luncheon, I just decided to surprise her. Honestly, I surprised myself! I went to the pet store and got all sorts of food and bowls and things before I even knew what I was doing. They're in the back with the catering equipment. I guess that's what the bowls are too! Catering equipment! Only now I'll be catering to you!"

Not for the first time, Ms. Trần laughed happily to herself. The same woman who had seemed so tired and reserved in the animal shelter had positively popped to life when she had gotten into the car with Nugget. Nugget's crate faced forward, so he couldn't see her as she drove; all he could see were the tops of trees and traffic lights sliding by as they wound their way through Boston. But he could hear the joy in her voice, and he could tell it was 100 percent sincere.

It was also contagious. Just like the breeze rolling in from where the passenger window had been cracked open, Ms. Trần was a breath of fresh air. After weeks of stormy mental weather, the dark clouds that had dominated Nugget's mind were slowly beginning to dissipate.

"And Emily deserves it," Ms. Trần continued. She appeared to be speaking a different language than she had spoken with the volunteer, but Nugget understood it perfectly as was the way of all dogs. "She works so hard at the restaurant— Oh, you're going to love the restaurant. But even when I tell her to go spend time with friends, she works and works! Such a nice girl, but, you know, I worry. So I thought, I should bring a friend to her! And when I saw you, I just knew you were perfect for her. For us."

And just like that, the dark clouds returned.

But why would you think that? How could I be perfect for anyone now? Didn't you see my face? It was the sort of downward thought spiral Nugget had become so used to that it didn't even feel like going downward anymore; it just felt like staying where he lived.

But Ms. Trần, unaware of the internal drama playing out in the passenger seat, continued to do something that would prove very shortly to be immensely important: She just kept on providing that breath of fresh air.

"Ooh, are you excited? We're almost there!"

And indeed, the air rushing into the car was now tinged with that faint but recognizable smell: chopped herbs and rich broth, floating hot on the wind and getting gradually closer, all mixed up with other delicious scents that Nugget couldn't even name yet.

The restaurant.

"Ah! Look at that!" Ms. Trần tutted, slowing the car down to gaze at something. "We open a little bit late, and already they've lined up outside. It'd be flattering if it wasn't costing us the customers who can't afford to wait. That's what I get for trying to run a family restaurant with just me and Emily. Well, and Mr. Adefolalu from the library, when he can pick up the extra shifts."

Ms. Trần waved out the window at a party Nugget couldn't see, and then drove on again, flicking her turn signal on at the end of the block.

"Let's go around the back," she said conspiratorially. "We can't have dogs out on the dining floor, even if everyone loves dogs."

Not me, said that familiar voice of doubt. *Everyone doesn't love me. Not anymore. And why would they? Why would Ms. Trần? She must be lying, or—*

And then another voice, one with cilantro on its breath, said: *If you'd stop thinking about yourself for a second, you'd notice Ms. Trần just said she runs a family restaurant with her daughter . . . and no one else. No Mr. Trần. Maybe you have more in common than you think.*

Huh. That was interesting. As Nugget's brain chewed on this thought like a rawhide, Ms. Trần pulled up to the back of her restaurant, where she parallel parked with an ease that would have put 95 percent of the world's automobile drivers to shame (unless those drivers had also spent many years running a small business in Boston out of the back of their car). Then she was out of the vehicle, circling the car, and opening the passenger door, lowering Nugget's crate to the ground and releasing him onto a cobblestone sidewalk behind a brick building. Nugget wasn't sure if Ms. Trần trusted him implicitly not to run away, or if she just didn't know you were supposed to put a dog on a leash. Either way, he wanted to impress her, so he sat and looked patiently up at her while she fished through the pockets of her puffy vest for keys to her building. Once she'd found them, she unlocked a thin door that swung open to reveal a hallway. At one end was another door, made of industrial steel; at the other end, a steep wooden staircase ascended upward to the entrance of an apartment. Linh and Emily Trần, Nugget realized, lived directly above their restaurant.

"Well!" Ms. Trần said, smiling down at Nugget affectionately. "After you."

It was a sign of how big Nugget had grown that he had no problem climbing these tall, rickety stairs, even though each one was taller than the carpeted steps that had given him so much trouble back in the Vandyck household.

And speaking of the Vandyck household: The closer they got to the door of the apartment, the more Nugget's heart filled with a feeling he thought he'd forgotten. It was the feeling of believing you might belong somewhere.

Then Ms. Trần was unlocking the upstairs door, and as she opened it, she yelled, "Emily! We're home!"

But there was no need to yell, because Emily was right there, emerging from behind the counter of a small kitchen unit. And as she did, that feeling of belonging spilled up and out of Nugget's heart, like water shot into a drinking glass from a fire hose.

There were many ways in which Emily Trần, at first glance, was different from Taylor Vandyck. She was a couple years older, looking to be fourteen to Taylor's twelve. Her black hair was cut in a bob, her bangs framing her brown eyes. *The same color as mine*, Nugget thought happily.

(He didn't even realize it was the first happy thought he'd had about his own appearance in weeks. This too would prove important.)

And whereas Taylor had been content spending most of her time either inside with the puppies or up in her room, Emily Trần was clearly someone who had places to be. She wore jeans covered in green grass stains, and a well-worn softball T-shirt bearing the same color of stains as the ones on her mother's clothes. Nugget was willing to bet those were the kinds of stains you got when you and your mom ran the best-smelling phở restaurant in Boston.

But there was one way in which Emily Trần reminded Nugget overwhelmingly of Taylor Vandyck: When she saw her mother, her face lit up. Here was someone who felt a fierce love for her family. Even though he had known her for exactly two seconds, Nugget could imagine himself returning that love just as fiercely.

Those two seconds were about to prove most important of all.

"Hey, Mom," Emily said. "I was waiting for you to get here before I let in any customers. Do you want help unloading the catering stuff? Or—"

Then Emily rounded the counter and saw Nugget.

She froze and stopped speaking midsentence. She looked back up at Ms. Trần, who was eagerly waiting for her daughter's reaction.

Her daughter's reaction was this: Emily's smile withered and died. The light in her eyes gave way to dark disbelief. The expression with which she beheld Nugget was still fierce, but it was not a loving fierceness. It looked on the surface like the disgust Nugget recognized all too well from his time at the animal shelter—but it was mixed with something deeper and even darker that Nugget did not yet know how to interpret.

"Is this a joke?" Emily spat.

Ms. Trần's own smile faltered. It returned again shortly, but now it was pained, twisted into a sad question mark.

"No, honey, of course not," she said. "I knew you wanted a dog, and when I went to the shelter today, I saw him and thought—well, I guess maybe I thought—"

"That's so messed up!" Emily shouted. "This is all messed up. Why can't one thing in my life be *normal*?"

"Emily, that is no way to—"

But Emily was already pushing past her mother and throwing open her bedroom door so hard that it bounced off the living room wall.

"I'm going to get ready for work!" Emily yelled. "I hope he's house-trained!"

And then she was out of sight, leaving Nugget and Ms. Trần alone together, standing stunned in the doorway of Nugget's new home.

28

(For the Record, He Was House-Trained)

In many ways, this was the worst-case scenario for Nugget. The exact thing he'd feared most had just come to pass: the seemingly inevitable rejection of him and his new, unignorable, unlovable face.

Indeed, any other young dog in Nugget's situation may have given up all hope.

But this was where all those important, soul-bolstering moments Nugget had just experienced in the car came into play. Those, and the fact that over the past few months, Nugget had lived a life like few other dogs, and loved like few other souls.

Because based on those two seconds alone, Nugget had decided with absolute certainty that Emily Trần was, on a fundamental level, a kind girl, even if her actions just now had been remarkably unkind. Nugget had learned that kind people could have all sorts of reasons for pushing newcomers away, even if all they really wanted was for someone to stay close to them. Yes, the hurt and shame he felt were real—but so was the fresh air he'd breathed in the car, and the way he'd felt as soon as he'd entered the Tràns' home, and the rising suspicion that there was a mystery to be solved here. Whatever had caused Emily to blow up like that, Nugget suspected it had been brewing long before he'd walked through the door. He could choose to focus on the shame he felt or he could focus on all those other things. And he had to imagine doing the latter would feel a lot better.

And he might even help Emily feel better in the process.

Right then and there, Nugget made a very big decision, one that would prove perhaps the most important moment of all. If family was the people you chose who chose you back, then surely sometimes you had to be the one to choose first.

Nugget padded toward Emily Tràn's room and lay down just outside it, waiting for her to come back out—not with the great running leaps he had once used to follow Taylor Vandyck to her room, but with the slow, sure confidence of someone who had just chosen his new family and was now willing to wait for them, somewhere on the other side of this mess, to choose him back. Or else . . .

Well, he just wouldn't think about *or else.*

A few minutes later, when Emily reemerged from her room, she nearly tripped over Nugget's curled-up form. At first, she cried out in aggrieved surprise.

But then she stopped and—in a voice so soft that only

Nugget's canine hearing could have caught it—grunted a secret. "Sorry."

And then she made her way down the stairs to work.

Nugget waited for the door at the bottom of the steps to open and close before he allowed himself—for the first time since that terrible moment when he'd looked in the mirror—to smile.

He stood up, stretched, and began to follow Emily Trần down the stairs.

And so Nugget began his life at Trần Phở.

29
Life at Trần Phở

Thwack-ack-ack!

"Three phở bò for the Võ family!"

"Coming up!"

Tangtangtang. Slapslapslap. Hisssssssss.

"Do you have—"

"I got it, Mom. Did you start on the—"

"The summer rolls, yes, just adding"—*chop*—"the shrimp"—*chop*—"now."

Dingdingding!

"Great, thanks, Mom. I'll go see who that is."

"Okay!" *Thwack-ack-ack-ack.* "I love y—"

But before Ms. Trần could even finish her sentence, Emily had shouldered her way through the double doors that separated the kitchen from the dining room floor, carrying a big tray on which mother and daughter had perfectly balanced three piping-hot bowls of phở. For the briefest of seconds, Ms. Trần stopped to gaze at the spot where her daughter had just been, the doors still lightly *thwack*-ing back and forth from the force with which Emily had pushed them apart.

Then another *ding* from outside signaled new customers coming in, and Ms. Trần went right back to work. She threw two more bowls on the crowded counter—*tangtang!*—dropped bright red beef slices into each one—*slapslap!*—and poured golden, steaming, aromatic beef broth on top, each bowl lined up seamlessly so that not a drop slopped out. Each slice of beef magically turned just the perfect shade of pink as the boiling broth cooked the raw meat. Ms. Trần had just enough time to chop and add a sprinkling of sprouts and spices before Emily was back in the kitchen, breathlessly calling out:

"Mr. and Mrs. Doherty—"

"I know," Ms. Trần said, turning and handing Emily the two bowls she had just prepared. "They always come this time on Tuesdays." Emily just grabbed the bowls, nodded, and muttered this information back to herself as if to burn it into her memory while she went backward out the door, and the whole dance started all over again.

The Trầns were pros. They were nonstop. They were a sight to behold.

And the whole time?

They didn't. Spill. *Anything.*

Nugget was torn between excruciation, admiration, and sheer sensory overload. He'd drooled his way through the entirety of the lunch rush, as Ms. Trần chopped, wrapped, scooped, stirred, and cut. He didn't know what was more impressive—how incredibly good Ms. Trần was at cooking, or how incredibly good Nugget was at hiding. Having quietly followed Emily downstairs and along the hall, Nugget stopped just outside the industrial steel door, remembering the words of the baker he'd met on the street all those weeks ago: "My boss would *not* want you in here *total* health code violation." He didn't want to get the Tràns in trouble, so he stayed hidden in the hallway. Thankfully, Emily had left the door ajar just a crack, so he was able to spy on the beautiful symphony of sounds and smells in the kitchen, all while perfectly hidden.

"You know I know you're there, yes?" Ms. Tràn asked.

Nugget looked around to see if Emily was there, but there was no one else. Weird. Ms. Tràn must have been talking to herself.

"Well, fine. Let me show you something." Ms. Tràn crossed the kitchen to a vat so big that it had to be holding fifty gallons of broth, minimum. Nugget shimmied his position to observe her closely, imagining the possibility of leftovers—surely she could afford to give a starving puppy at least, like, *twenty* gallons.

"You see how it looks completely calm?" Ms. Tràn said, stirring the golden broth with a huge ladle. "Well, you have to be careful. You can't bother me when I'm over here. Everything in here is boiling hot."

Nugget tilted his head. It didn't *look* like anything was boiling. He could *smell* the heat radiating off the vat even from out in the hall, but the surface of the liquid was completely smooth.

"I know it looks like nothing is happening," Ms. Trần began, "but that's just because all the fat has risen to the surface. The fat is heavier than the water, so it forms a sort of lid that blocks you from seeing what's happening beneath it, where all the wonderful flavors and juices have been stewing for hours."

Nugget's eyes widened in anticipation, unsure what would happen next.

"You can't let the appearance fool you. That's dangerous," Ms. Trần warned. "But if you look through to what's underneath . . ." She skimmed a big scoop off the surface with her ladle, and a mouthwatering scent exploded into the room like a genie escaping from a lamp. "*That's* where all the best things are."

She smiled like she had just said something important. Maybe she had. Nugget was still kind of focused on what was going on with the ladle.

Then Emily burst through the doors.

"One bánh xèo!" she called out, and immediately she was gone again.

Right! That was the other thing Nugget was supposed to be focusing on. Spying on the kitchen was thrilling, but it wasn't helping him get any closer to Emily or to solving the mystery of what had come between her and her mother. As long as Emily was working front of house, Nugget's only real hope of spending time with her was to follow her out onto the main floor of the restaurant, which he absolutely wasn't supposed to do.

And anyway, every time he thought about it, he had a vision of the patrons outside, chatting happily, enjoying their food . . . until Nugget emerged through the double doors. First, one set of eyes would fall on him, then another, and another, until everyone in the restaurant would be staring in horror at the noseless dog, and no one would have any appetite whatsoever, and then the business would be ruined.

Nugget could see it all clearly, and it made his stomach churn. In fact, it was almost enough to put him off *his* appetite, which for Nugget was really saying something. Seeking comfort, he subconsciously started to creep closer to the door.

"Ah ah ah," Ms. Trần began to warn, causing Nugget to freeze just as Emily burst back in and said, "We need three—Oh, come *on*, Mom! He can*not* come in here!"

"You know what?" Ms. Trần looked up at her daughter and smiled. "You're absolutely right. He needs to get out of here and into the fresh air. And so do you!"

Emily tensed up instantly, her shoulders hitching up around her ears. "No, I don't."

"According to Massachusetts state law," Ms. Trần said drily, "you really do. And you can take— Wait a second. It's

Tuesday! You have field hockey on Tuesdays! Were you just not going to say anything about it?"

Emily visibly strained not to whip her head around as from the front of the house another *ding* announced more customers arriving.

"I don't need to go," she said. "I can skip practice. You need help here."

"*You* need to *play*," Ms. Trần said firmly. "All kids do."

"Fine!" Emily threw her hands up. "Then I guess I can't walk the dog!"

"Why not?"

"I can't just take him to the athletic field with me! There's sticks and balls flying everywhere, and it's busy, and he'd hate it!"

I'd love that! Nugget thought urgently.

"He'd love that!" Ms. Trần smiled. Nugget *really* liked Ms. Trần.

Emily made one last weak attempt as her mother crossed behind her in the cramped kitchen aisle.

"How can I take him with me? I don't even know his name."

"They didn't tell me a name," Ms. Trần said, concentrating on something behind Emily's shoulder. "What a perfect chance for you to think of one while you get to know each other better."

She stepped back. With one smooth move, she had untied

the back of Emily's apron and handed her Nugget's leash. She had also produced a bag of athletic equipment from somewhere in a cupboard that Nugget hadn't even seen her open or shut. In her own kitchen, there was nothing Ms. Trần could not do.

Which was how Emily Trần found herself being pulled out the back of the building by an eager Nugget, off to a world where they knew each other better and away from the bustle of Trần Phở.

Ding!

30
The Captains of Ronan Park

Within just a few minutes, Nugget had already learned several fascinating things about Emily Trần.

"Could you slow down? You don't even know where we're going. *I* know where we're going. *You* should be following *me*."

For one thing, she talked to Nugget just as much as her mother did when they were alone—albeit in a slightly different tone.

"Of course, the faster we get to practice, the faster we can get back to helping Mom. So that's something, I guess."

That was another fascinating thing: For a girl who apparently played field hockey, owned a bunch of field hockey equipment, and wore shirts covered in just the kind of grass stains you'd get if you were really enthusiastically playing field hockey . . . Emily didn't seem that excited to go to field hockey.

Nugget pondered these things as Emily led them up a weedy sidewalk to the crest of a hill, where a green and multi-leveled park revealed itself, rolling down the other side of the hill in stages, like an enormous grassy staircase that descended all the way to the eternal blue shine of Boston Harbor below. Etched into the concrete base of a flagpole were the words RONAN PARK, and on the far side of that flagpole was a field full of girls wearing thick gloves and running shoes. Each girl ran at full tilt across the grass, brandishing J-shaped sticks in pursuit of a whizzing white ball.

Field hockey practice was already in full swing.

This was when Nugget suddenly went from learning a few things about Emily to learning a *lot*.

The moment the other girls came into view, Nugget's nose was on *fire* with the smell of fear. It was coming, he quickly realized, from Emily, who positively crackled with the smell like an emergency flare shooting sparks into the air.

And it wasn't just any fear either. It was the fear very specifically of being seen. Nugget recognized it because he had felt that fear himself. He'd felt it every day back at Father Patrick's Last Chance Animal Shelter, and, if he was being honest, he was feeling it now as the two of them slowly approached the playing field, each one more reluctant than the other to advance. It was the kind of fear that said "Please don't notice me. Please don't look at me. Please don't—"

But that was the worst thing about this fear: It always came true.

"Hey, Trần! You're late!"

A girl a couple years older than Emily jogged over,

her sandy brown ponytail bouncing behind her. She wore a maroon jersey that read GORGONS. A couple feet above Nugget's head, Emily's knuckles squeezed so tightly around the handle of his leash that Nugget could feel the physical tug of her distress.

"I'm sorry, Madison," Emily said. "I was helping my—"

"Sorry isn't gonna win us any matches." This came from another sandy-haired girl who had also peeled away from practice. They weren't twins—Nugget would have smelled it if they were related—but between their ponytails and their uniforms, they looked nearly identical.

"Lexington is right," said Madison. "You need to start prioritizing— *Oh*, my *God*, what is *that*?!"

And now everyone's fears had come true.

The two girls had finally noticed Nugget.

At Father Patrick's, some of the visiting families had had the decency to try not to stare at Nugget's nose, or rather, his lack thereof. Or maybe those families weren't being decent. Maybe they just didn't want to look again and risk catching a second glimpse of the terrible thing they thought they'd just seen out of the corner of their eyes. Whatever the reason, it had worked fine for Nugget.

Well, no. It had felt terrible. But it had been better than somebody openly gawking in horror.

The girls, though? Born to gawk. International, first-class gawk stars. Their jaws dropped. Their eyes widened. Madison even took a step back, as if Nugget was somehow contagious. It all made Nugget want to bury himself, to hide himself from the light. But here on this wide, flat field there was nowhere to go—and Emily's tight grip on the leash wouldn't have let him go anyway.

"It's—he's—a dog." Emily's words were stiff, like each one had been clinging to her teeth before she forcibly pushed them out of her mouth.

"God. Wow." Lexington made a sound somewhere between a gasp and a laugh. "Are you sure? What's its name?"

"He doesn't have one yet."

This time, when Madison made a sound, there was no mistake: It was a laugh. And not a nice one.

"You should call it Ugly," she said.

It was at this point that Nugget sort of broke in two.

One part of him was still standing there, still living through his worst nightmare, still looking up helplessly while these two girls made him feel the smallest he had ever felt.

The other part of him, though—much quieter, yes, but still a real, distinct part with a soft and persistent voice—was watching all this from a distance. And that part was whispering: *You know, Ms. Trần didn't react this way when she saw you. She was kind. Even Emily didn't* laugh *at you.*

Which then led to the next thought: *Maybe someone being this mean says more about* them *than it does about* me.

It was an odd thought, but it sat there at the bottom of

Nugget's mind, as if waiting for him to sniff at it later when he was ready.

And then something even odder happened: Emily seemed to have the exact same thought.

"Yeah," Lexington was saying, "you should totally—"

"*You* should mind your own business!" Emily blurted. "And *he's* not an *it!*"

This outburst seemed to surprise everyone involved, Emily most of all.

"Well," Lexington intoned, her words ice-cold. "If that's how you want to talk to your team captains."

"I—I didn't—" Emily stammered.

"Whatever," Madison interjected. "We're about to start a scrimmage—but you can start by taking the bench."

"But . . ." Despair rolled off Emily in waves. "But I took the bench last time."

"And? You were late last time too." Madison shook her head as she continued to back away toward the field, pretending to look disappointed. But Nugget could smell the truth, and the truth was that she wasn't disappointed at all. She'd wanted this to happen.

"Honestly, Trân. I don't know how you ever hope to improve if you keep this behavior up. What if we have to cut you from the team?"

As one, the two captains turned and took to the field, leaving Emily alone with Nugget.

"Now look at the mess we're in," Emily grumbled.

But in a direct reversal of Madison's deception, Emily wasn't actually angry. She really *did* smell of pure, unleaded disappointment. And there was no blame in her eyes for Nugget. She wasn't even looking at him as she spoke.

She only had eyes for the field and all the happy girls on it, each preparing to play some hockey.

Wait.

Shoot.

We need to talk about field hockey.

31

Hockey(s)

You have probably heard of hockey. Even Nugget knew about it. Mr. Vandyck, Mrs. Vandyck, and, perhaps most vocally, Lucky the porcupine had all been devoted fans of the Boston Bruins, so the subject had come up before.

But the Bruins played ice hockey, not field hockey. Ice hockey, of course, is a fun and popular game in which people strap knives to their feet in order to move at alarmingly high speeds using big, heavy, L-shaped sticks to slap a piece of rubber around at even higher speeds in the hopes that the rubber will go into the opposing team's goal or, failing that, someone's mouth.

Field hockey is just like that, except for all the ways in which it is different.

Instead of knives, players make the much more sensible decision to wear cleats. Instead of a flat puck, the rubber everyone is chasing around takes the form of a bright white ball. And while the sticks are still big and heavy, they are not L-shaped, but rather J-shaped—a design that better allows players to trap the ball in the curve of their sticks before dribbling or shooting it at wicked speeds toward the goal.

Oh, and it takes place on a field. That's a really big part of field hockey. It's difficult to overemphasize how important it is that field hockey be played on a field.

And it's not just because it's in the name either. The physical fact of the field shapes not just the game of field hockey but the kind of person who chooses to play. On ice skates, a hockey player can glide across their rink in seconds. But the girls of the Ronan Park Gorgons had only their cleats and the solid ground beneath their feet. If they wanted to keep up with the ball, they had to *run*—fast, hard, and long. These girls were young, but each one of them possessed more stamina and endurance than some adults would ever achieve.

And now, in front of the longing eyes of both Emily and Nugget, all that strength and stamina was being put to remarkable use. One moment the ball would be on the far end of the field, racing toward the goal at a speed that helped explain why the goalkeepers were wearing shin pads roughly the size and shape of aerodynamic, fashionable trash can lids. Then, just before the ball could reach the goal, a fullback on the defensive line would stop the ball with her stick, cradling it gently for a split second before dribbling it forward and whipping it back from whence it came in a merciless driving pass.

If the simple pleasures of Ms. Trần's kitchen had been

excruciating, this was sheer torture. Nugget, after all, was a dog, and any dog watching this spectacle would have wanted one thing only: to run out there and play. Each time the ball shot past—and it shot past a *lot* of times—Nugget had to stop himself from leaping after it. Especially when an overly enthusiastic player sent the ball flying out of bounds and the whole game had to stop while someone ran to grab it.

You guys know I'm right here, right? Nugget wanted to ask. *Born to fetch. There's a technique to it. Hard to explain, of course. Best if I just show you.*

But what was really interesting was that each time he felt tempted to pull the leash one way or the other to follow the action . . . the leash would give way just slightly, as if moving in tandem with him. It took Nugget several quarters to realize what was going on, but when he did, it struck him right in the heart.

Emily was also subconsciously moving her body in the direction of the ball.

She wanted to be out there as badly as Nugget did. Maybe worse.

And then at the very end of the practice, just when all hope seemed lost . . . it looked like she might get her chance.

"Emily Trần!"

Emily leaped up as a tall woman in a windbreaker strode toward her.

"Yes, Coach Farineau?"

"I didn't even notice you arrive!" The coach seemed genuinely apologetic. "Have you gotten to play yet today?"

"No, Coach."

"Well, go ahead and get in there—"

"Excuse me? Coach Farineau?"

It was Lexington. Or was it Madison? Nugget had already forgotten which one smelled like which.

"Somebody needs to collect the cones," she said.

"Oh. I suppose they do." Coach Farineau gazed over the field, frowning at the harbor in the distance, and then looked regretfully back at Emily. "I don't suppose you'd mind—"

"Of course not, Coach Farineau," Emily muttered.

She slouched off, performing the obligatory grunt work that closed every field hockey practice and dragging Nugget along after her. Then, after tossing the cones unceremoniously at the edge of the field, she kept slouching, all the way out of Ronan Park and back down the hill to Trần Phở.

Upon reaching the storefront of Trần Phở, Emily paused, and Nugget paused with her. They stood just out of view of the restaurant's front window, but Nugget could hear the sound of bowls clinking and clanking and happy customers talking and slurping. There was a world of warmth and community waiting for Emily inside.

But she just lowered her head and, heaving her equipment bag over her shoulder one more time, took Nugget around the back of the restaurant and into the hallway, where she moved to pull Nugget silently up the stairs before anyone could hear them.

The fear of being seen could be hard to shake.

It also continued to be totally futile.

"Emily! Come here! How was your practice? Did you two have a good time?"

Through the door at the end of the hall, Ms. Trần beamed expectantly from over a pot of brisket, waiting for Emily's reply, which didn't seem to be coming.

Tell her! Nugget urged Emily, butting his head against her ankle. *Tell her those girls were mean to you! Tell her they won't let you play with them!*

But the now familiar pull of Emily's grip tightening around his leash made Nugget look up at her and then follow her gaze to where she was looking: right at her mother.

And for the first time, Nugget saw Ms. Trần through Emily's eyes: That tired smile only looked more tired with every hour. She had changed, at some point, from her broth-splashed apron into a still-broth-splashed-but-slightly-less-broth-splashed apron; presumably the kind you wore if you were trying to work both front of house *and* the kitchen all afternoon while your daughter selfishly went off to her own activities, where she wasn't even *participating* in said activities, which said daughter just knew would break your heart if she told you. Or, worse, get you all fired up to go and speak to someone about it, causing you to put your entire livelihood on an even longer pause than you had already done just to stop the constant motion of your restaurant and ask your daughter how her day was.

And so it made a terrible sense when Emily just said: "It was fine. He pooped."

Well, it was a bit rude to talk about Nugget's private life like that.

But. Still. It made sense.

Ms. Trần, though, was not so easily fooled.

"You know, if something's wrong, you can always—"

"Nothing's wrong." Emily dropped Nugget's leash and hurried into the kitchen, already throwing on an apron, seemingly forgetting all about Nugget in her rush to change the subject. "I'm sorry for blowing up earlier. Here, let me help you with—"

Then, in her hurry to tie her apron strings in the tight quarters of the kitchen, Emily knocked an onion off the prep counter with her elbow.

It is in moments like this that a dog's five senses switch instantaneously into overdrive, along with developing a few extra senses besides, one of which is the slowing of time. Did Nugget really *want* to eat an entire raw onion, per se? Not *necessarily*, no. But it was human food, and it was falling to the ground, and there's just certain things you have to do on principle as a dog, like moving heaven and Earth by bounding down a hallway to meet that food when it hits the ground.

But.

Of all the things in heaven and Earth, it turned out Emily Trần was the only thing faster than a hungry dog. In a movement so swift, Nugget may not have processed it if he was not, again, currently throwing himself across the floor in slow motion, Emily cinched her apron with one hand, grabbed a pair of tongs from above her head with the other, swirled in a graceful arc, snatched the onion deftly out of midair with the tongs, cradled it as gently as an uncooked egg to make sure it did not bruise, and, in the completion of her 360-degree twirl, tossed the onion with perfect aim and accuracy directly to Ms. Trần, who caught the onion with both hands in a combination of instinct and surprise, much like the surprise that Nugget felt as he skidded to a halt in the hall.

Time resumed its normal speed.

"Okay," Emily said nonchalantly, chucking the tongs aside as if she had not just used them to perform wonders and miracles. "I'm gonna go out on the floor. Love you, Mom."

She pushed through the double doors and was gone.

"I just don't know what to do about that girl," Ms. Trần sighed to Nugget, rolling the onion absentmindedly from one hand to the other. Nugget stared at the onion—and not just because he was still hungry. Something very important had just fallen into place.

That's okay, he was trying to tell Ms. Trần. *You don't have to do anything. I'm going to do it for you.*

32
Fetch Happens

Nugget didn't have to wait very long for his chance to act.

The very next day, Emily had practice again. The moment she hauled her equipment bag out from the kitchen, Nugget not-so-subtly ran in circles around it, as if warming himself up to play field hockey. This time when Ms. Trần suggested Emily bring Nugget along to practice, Emily just sighed and went to grab his leash. Nugget counted this as progress.

"Have you thought of a name for him yet?" Ms. Trần asked as Emily bent down to clip the leash to his collar.

"Why don't *you* think of a name for him?"

Okay, maybe not so much progress.

"Because I want it to be something special for the two of you."

Kneeling there on the ground with Nugget, Emily paused as if she wanted to say something. But then she just wrapped the leash tight around her wrist, stood, and headed out the door with dog and duffel bag in tow.

This time they arrived at practice just as it was beginning, so Emily was able to tie Nugget up to a bleacher post and join her teammates in stretches, box drills, and tackle practice. But when the time came to split up into teams for a scrimmage, Madison (or was it Lexington?) sidled over to Emily and hissed in her ear.

No one else on the field would have heard it. Coach Farineau, giving passing pointers to a sweeper, wasn't even looking. Only Nugget, with his canine hearing, was able to hear the singular word, carried on the breeze that blew over the hilltop.

"Bench."

And so only Nugget was able to witness what he was beginning to recognize as a habit for Emily. A dark cloud passed across her face like she was going to say something . . . but then, when she opened her mouth, nothing came out, and when she closed it again, it was as if she had swallowed the dark cloud whole and was choking on the lightning and hail as it went down.

One silver lining: At least she untied Nugget from the bleachers when she came over to heave herself onto the bench, settling in for another day of disappointment. The untying appeared to be an unconscious act for Emily, something she did so she could continue to knead at the leash handle. But it meant everything to Nugget.

Because for Nugget, the day was just beginning.

Just like last time, Nugget watched the ball go back and forth, his eyes locked onto its movements like it might disappear at any second. But he didn't want it to disappear. He wanted it to—

There! There it was! The sweeper who had needed passing pointers earlier had just attempted a long-distance pass—and accidentally sent the ball flying out of bounds.

But this time, Nugget went flying too.

"Hey!" Emily cried, but Nugget had taken her by surprise. His leash slid right out of her hand, flapping behind him in the wind. Nugget was running fast, and Emily was already in hot pursuit along with half the girls on the team. They put up a good chase—they were athletes, after all—but as Nugget saw it, it was simple math: Four legs were twice as fast as two. Within moments, Nugget leaped through the air and—*pock!*—had the ball in his mouth.

It was Nugget's first time catching something with his new mouth, and his first feeling was one of unspeakable relief—the revelation that he still *could* catch; that his teeth, snaggly though they looked, were still perfect for snagging toys.

The second feeling was that this was not your average toy. The ball reeked of cork and rubber—rubber with a licorice tang so strong that you almost had to wonder: Did rubber, actually, taste like licorice? Or did all licorice just taste like rubber?

The third and final feeling was centuries of *Canis familiaris* instinct flooding Nugget's body. The yelling of the humans; the ball in his teeth; in the grand tradition of dog-human relations, this was the holy moment in which he would turn around and return the ball to them. It was the eternal promise of fetch: What goes out must come back.

But Nugget did not come back. He went wide, arcing north by northeast, away from everyone who followed him.

Well, *almost* everyone. Due to her unique starting point on the bench, the only person who had any chance of catching him now was Emily. But even then, she would have to be extraordinarily fast to do it.

This was tricky. Nugget didn't want to make this look too easy for her, but he also didn't want her to fail.

As it turned out, he needn't have worried. With the agility of someone who had spent every day this summer up on her feet running a restaurant, Emily banked north, closing the distance between her and the fugitive dog at a pace that surprised even the dog in question. What was more, at some point Emily had snatched up a hockey stick just as deftly as she'd grabbed those tongs in the kitchen. Now she brought the stick down in front of Nugget so quickly that he had to rear up on his hind legs and turn to avoid stumbling right over it.

But the stick was already in front of Nugget again, forcing him to change direction a second time. And then again, and again, as Emily ran alongside him, somehow not just keeping up with an energetic puppy but guiding him back toward the field, *herding* him, like she was a shepherd and the hockey stick her staff.

In fact, as the stick reversed position back and forth on either side of him, Nugget realized he wasn't just being herded. Without ever actually touching him, Emily was using the stick to *dribble* Nugget.

For a moment, the din of the girls dropped away as they tried to process what they were seeing.

Then, one girl—the same one who had sent the ball flying in the first place—pumped her fists up and yelled, "Go, Trần!"

That was followed by a *"Yeah!"* from the midfield line. Suddenly, everyone was chiming in:

"You got this!"

"Woo-hoo!"

"Great stickwork, Emily!"

That last one came from Coach Farineau. *Perfect.* As Nugget approached the field, he knew he had to get his next few steps just right.

So he tripped over his own paws and skidded across the grass.

It was flawless. Just as he'd planned. The ball looked completely natural popping out of his mouth, and the Gorgons gasped as it seemed for a moment like Emily was going to trample over the defenseless little puppy.

Emily just gritted her teeth, sidestepped the four-legged obstacle in front of her, brought her right hand up to join her left at the top of the stick, and, with a mighty swing, slammed

the ball right down the middle of the field at the goalkeeper—
who grabbed the ball out of the air and tore off her face mask
to reveal a speechless Lexington as the entire team went wild.

"Wow, Emily," said Coach Farineau. "I had no idea you
had those kinds of chops in you. How come we haven't seen
that before?"

Emily shrugged humbly, but the scent of exhilaration was
all over her.

"I guess I haven't had the chance," she said.

"Well, we'll have to fix that." Coach Farineau called out
to the field. "Madison!"

"Yes, Coach?" Madison stood in the center of the forward line, as stunned as her co-captain.

"You're doing great today. Take a break. Emily's gonna
sub in. And let's make sure she's on the starting forward line
next week!"

"Yes, Coach." However Madison felt in that moment,
her face indicated it was the equal and exact opposite of how
Emily and Nugget felt.

"Great!" Coach clapped her hands and turned back to
them. "This'll be wonderful, Emily. I guess it's a good thing
you brought your dog to— Oh, dear."

Nugget's elation was briefly punctured as Coach looked
down and saw him clearly for the first time. He lowered his
ears flat around his skull, but big as they were, he still couldn't
hide his face.

"I'm sorry," Coach Farineau said, attempting to recover. "I just didn't . . . notice. What's the, uh—What's their name?"

"I haven't decided yet," said Emily.

And then she added something that made Nugget's ears perk back up.

"But I'm thinking about it."

As the coach instructed the girls to get back in position, Emily led Nugget back to the post on the side of the field, kneeling down to tie him up extra securely this time. But now, as her hands nimbly tied the leash into a knot, she looked Nugget right in the face, as if she was searching for something—a hint, an acknowledgment that what he'd done had been on purpose.

Of course, Nugget's face was uniquely hard to read these days.

But still, Emily looked right at him. No flinching. No wincing. Just probing assessment as if she were seeing him with new eyes.

And that gave Nugget the strength to not flinch either. Rather than moving his ears down, or turning away, he just let himself be looked at—and he looked back in turn.

A girl and a dog saw each other.

"Emily! Match is starting!"

The game began.

33

Sticks and Stones

After that, the days started to fly by.

It made sense; time flies when you're enjoying yourself, and that's exactly what Nugget was doing. Each morning, he woke to Ms. Trần pouring a delicious breakfast into his bowl, and each morning, Ms. Trần made the same joke about how little her newest catering client was paying her. Then she would laugh as if someone had just told the joke to her for the first time, every time. Nugget would have happily laughed with her if he wasn't so busy eating.

After that, he'd get a nice long walk around the neighborhood. Ms. Trần liked to crisscross up and down the many alleys and back avenues around her home, presumably for some shade from the summer heat. This worked great for Nugget, who enjoyed that this route ensured as few horrified onlookers as possible. There was something about Ms. Trần's clear, unquestioned delight in Nugget's company that boosted his confidence just a little—but not so much that he wanted to put it to the test.

Before he could dwell too long on that, though, they'd be

right back at the restaurant, firing up the kitchen for the day ahead, sometimes even allowing Nugget to watch as long as his leash was tied to the banister of the staircase out in the hall, well away from the food preparation area. Some days, it was just Ms. Trần and Emily, washing and blanching the ingredients they'd prepared the night before. Other days, though, they were joined by Mr. Adefolalu, a tall man with a booming laugh and glasses that fogged up every time he stood near any bowl of phở, which was to say often. Nugget liked Mr. Adefolalu, whose first reaction to seeing Nugget's face was not to look away *or* to stare, but simply to smile and say, "Linh tells me you fought a lion. Very cool, buddy. *Very* cool."

Huh. When you put it like that, it *did* sound kind of cool.

Then the lunch rush would begin, and life in the kitchen would take on its familiar frenzied pace for the rest of the day until closing time, when Mr. Adefolalu would wash dishes while Ms. Trần got tomorrow's menu started and Emily took Nugget for his evening walk. At first Emily's walks were short affairs; she would pretty much lead Nugget up the avenue and back again, trying to return to the kitchen as fast as possible to help out, sometimes even muttering all the ingredients they had to order that night to herself. Nugget found that this walking style left something to be desired, even if it was kind of a nice change of pace to have people on the sidewalk move away from them not because they were trying to avoid the hideous, noseless dog—who they couldn't really see in the dim evening light anyway—but because they were trying to avoid the grumpy young girl talking to herself as she stalked down the avenue.

But as the days went on, Nugget noticed Emily starting to relax. Their walks lasted longer and Emily's choice of walking paths grew more winding, as if she was unconsciously mimicking her mother. And rather than simply grumbling to herself, she started occasionally asking Nugget's opinion on things, like "What do you think customers would like better? More shallots, or more roast ginger? Don't act like you don't have an opinion—I've seen you drooling at both."

Or "Did you see that smoothie place's chalkboard specials display? Sloppy. I've been doing better chalk since I was eight. I mean, I was *super* into chalk when I was eight, so it's not really fair, but still. Poor guys. Do you think they'd pay me to save them from themselves?"

Pretty soon, they were regularly getting back well after nightfall, and while Emily would always volunteer to help put things away, Ms. Trần would insist that her daughter be done working for the night.

One night, after Emily eventually gave in and went upstairs, Ms. Trần emerged from the kitchen just long enough to look thoughtfully down at Nugget.

"You're very good for her, you know," she said. "Her taking breaks? That's new. And you're new. So it must be you. And that's good."

And then—wonder of wonders—she tossed Nugget a rice noodle and went back to cleaning while Nugget chewed and wagged his tail happily.

After all, Ms. Trần may have been right. The increasing length of Emily and Nugget's evening walks was directly correlated to the increase in time Emily was spending on the playing field at Ronan Park, and Nugget felt very proud of the part he'd played in making that happen. By the end of the first week, Emily had been on the starting lineup for every practice. By the next week, Coach Farineau had asked her to help lead drills in drag flicking and push passing. Emily, normally so intent on hiding her emotions, came home from these practices wearing an unguarded smile on her face, which brightened Ms. Trần's smile as well.

And while she still hadn't given Nugget a name, it had been weeks since Emily had had to be reminded to bring him to practice. After the "fetch" incident, Emily had taken the initiative on every practice day to get Nugget's leash out before she even got out her equipment bag. The other girls still weren't sure what to make of the dog with the distinctive features, and Nugget had noticed them hanging back from the bleachers whenever he was tied there. But while this hurt, he tried to focus on the positive: A few of the girls were clearly warming to Emily, and that warmed Nugget's heart as well.

But not everyone was thrilled about Emily's rise. If Lexington and Madison had been hostile toward Emily

before, the fact that she was now eating into what they per-
ceived as *their* playing time had only caused their resentments
to grow. And they weren't above using their positions as
co-captains to make their feelings known. Their passes to her
were always a little harder than necessary; her share of the
assigned grunt work always a little more than everyone else's.
It was just enough that Coach Farineau wouldn't have noticed
without being told—and Emily would never tell her. For the
simple reason that . . .

Well, sometimes Nugget wanted to ask Emily what her
reasons were. Here, firsthand, was a lesson in how it looked
to choose someone over and over, only for them not to choose
you back. If he could have, Nugget would have asked her
why: why she kept doing this to herself, why she didn't just
tell someone what was going on, why she wanted so badly to
belong *here* when there were other people out there who would
accept her just as she was.

But on some level . . . Nugget knew. He knew all too
well what it felt like to want to belong somewhere so badly
that you would overlook any amount of indignity, of rejection, of getting knocked down. He knew what it felt like to
get right back up again because maybe *this* time it would all
work out.

The tricky thing was that this wasn't always bad.
Persistence and hard work can be great qualities. But it is
important to make sure you're working toward the *right* things.

Throw yourself at a closed door and you're likely to get hurt before the door does. Get pushed down too many times and something is going to break.

For Emily, that break came on August the ninth.

It was a humid day at the top of Ronan Park. Heat shimmered over the water of the bay below. The Gorgons were all in the midst of a well-earned break, sprawled out around the field and gulping water from insulated bottles the size of small vacuum cleaners. Emily had collapsed on the grass next to Nugget, which had surprised him; sitting near Nugget was pretty much a guarantee that no other girls would sit near Emily, so even though he knew this probably should not have been where he set the bar, Nugget still appreciated the small show of solidarity.

Today, though, a few girls actually followed Emily over to the bleachers: Shanna, the sweeper from that fateful practice all those weeks ago, and Katie, a goalkeeper with the happy, easygoing air of someone who had managed to turn "mostly just standing around" into an athletic pursuit.

"Oh, you don't have to—" Emily began, but Katie waved her hand in a good-natured dismissal of Emily's concerns.

"We want to!"

"Yeah," Shanna said, smiling at Emily and then at Nugget. "We want to get to know you more. And this is technically the only boy ever to catch one of my pop-ups. What's his name anyway?"

Despite herself, Emily smiled and quickly untied Nugget's leash from the bleachers post.

"Well," she said. "Actually—"

"His name is Ugly."

A shadow fell over Emily's face—literally. Lexington had planted herself above the girls, standing directly between them and the sun, leaning on her hockey stick, and looking down at them all.

Nugget heard Emily's heart start to race. But he also saw Katie, facing away from Lexington, roll her eyes—and Emily must have seen this too because she was suddenly emboldened to swallow her fear and say, "Don't call him that."

"Why?" Madison asked innocently, suddenly appearing at Lexington's side—or had she been there the whole time? "It's not like you've given Ugly a real name yet."

"Madison—" Shanna began, but the captain shot her a look that stopped her instantly. Emily was not the only team member who feared these girls.

"I said," Emily repeated, more slowly this time, "don't. Call him. Ugly."

"So you *do* like him?" Lexington asked. "I wasn't sure. You seemed embarrassed of him before. But I guess you actually wouldn't be that embarrassed by stuff looking weird. My dad went to your restaurant once and he said he couldn't tell what he was eating. Even your *food* is ugl—"

"HE'S NOT UGLY!"

One girl threw herself forward, and four girls and a dog threw themselves backward, as Emily burst from the ground with that same speed and ferocity that made her so darn good at field hockey. Now, though, that speed became a liability; before anyone could grab a hold of Emily or talk her out of losing her composure, she'd already hurtled into Madison, sending the co-captain to the ground with a shriek and a *thud*.

"*Hey!*"

Coach Farineau, of course, had not seen or heard any of the lead-up to the shove; she had only noticed the shove itself, and it brought her running.

"Trần, what are you *doing?*"

Emily stood over Madison, panting, looking around wildly as she regained her senses.

"I didn't—she kept—"

"This kind of behavior is unacceptable," Coach Farineau said, helping a shaken Madison up off the ground.

As always, Emily looked like she wanted to say something; as always, Emily faltered.

Advocate for yourself! Nugget thought. *You deserve to be treated well! You don't have to keep all your pain a secret!*

But at last, Emily just said, "Sorry, Coach," and ran off down the hill, leaving Nugget to run after her.

34
Being Honest

For the first time ever, Emily returned from field hockey practice and *didn't* go straight into the kitchen to throw on her apron. Instead she pounded up the wooden stairs to the Tràns' apartment, where Nugget had just enough time to slip through the apartment door on Emily's heels before she slammed it shut behind her and ran to her bedroom, slamming *that* door too for good measure.

This was not Nugget's first time dealing with a sad human. It wasn't even his first time dealing with a tween girl crying alone in her room. This was not the sort of thing he had hoped to become an expert in, but what were you going to do?

Well, that was the question, wasn't it? What *was* Nugget going to do? The last time this had happened, he'd thrown himself into helping Taylor Vandyck, barging right into her room and licking her face until she'd laughed and felt better. But this time, he was held back by a fear: What if being licked by *this* face, Nugget's new half face, just made Emily feel worse instead of better? Especially when it had arguably been the very thing to get her in trouble in the first place?

Luckily after a few moments of Nugget hesitating, Emily made the decision for him. She emerged from her room, wiped the back of her hand across her eyes, and looked bleariily down at Nugget.

"Get in here, doofus," she said. Then, before Nugget could respond, she turned and made her way back into her room, collapsing into bed with an audible *oomph* and all the while leaving the door open.

He'd take it.

Nugget had never actually been in Emily's room before. It smelled like her, of course, but also like pine-scented candles, and, indeed, thanks to a well-decorated blackboard atop her dresser, like chalk. The walls were decorated with posters of Olympic athletes and photos of the Trần family. Nugget had just jumped up into bed after Emily when there was a knock at the doorway, followed by Ms. Trần slowly easing the door further open.

"Honey? I thought I heard you— *Oh*," she said, seeing her daughter furiously rubbing at her face and refusing to look at her.

Then she saw Nugget.

"Well," Ms. Trần said, "this is progress."

This, at least, got Emily to look at her mother.

"What are you *talking* about?" she asked.

"I know that you don't always want to let me in when something's wrong," Ms. Trần sighed. "But I'm glad you've started to let him in, at least."

"Nothing's wrong!" Emily spat, though she might have been more convincing if her face and pillow hadn't been streaked with tears.

"You see what I mean?" Ms. Trần sat on the bed, putting her arm around Emily. "I know when I'm not being told the truth."

Pressed up against her as he was, Nugget could feel Emily stiffen up in her mother's embrace.

"You're one to talk," she muttered.

"What?" Ms. Trần smelled like surprise.

"You act like the restaurant doesn't exhaust you, but I know it does. How am I supposed to bother you with my stuff when you've already got so much to deal with?"

"Well— I—" Ms. Trần searched desperately for the right words. "The only thing that *might* bother me is when you shut me out, so . . . you're failing either way!"

Emily threw her hands up, knocking off her mom's arm. "Oh, so now I'm a failure no matter what I do?!"

"What?! No! I've worked incredibly hard—"

"I know you have!"

"—to never make you feel that way! The way my—the way other mothers can make *their* daughters feel!"

Nugget's head whipped between mother and daughter.

"Well, it happened anyway!" Emily yelled. "So maybe sometimes we should just hash these things out like other mothers and daughters, rather than just *pretending* everything's normal!"

"Well, maybe we *should*!" Ms. Trần yelled back.

And then they both stopped yelling and stared at each other, each seemingly winded by their own outburst. Nugget had never seen Ms. Trần flustered like this. It seemed like Emily hadn't either. The surprise seemed to embolden her—and her mother.

"If something is going on with your friends—" Ms. Trần pressed at last.

"I don't have any friends."

The confession sat in the air, between the two humans, just above Nugget's head.

"That's why I want to do so much for the restaurant, and prove myself to the Gorgons. That's the only time I feel like people like me."

But in that moment, Emily did something she'd never really done before: She began to pet Nugget, slowly and surely, dragging her fingers through the fur on the back of his head, smoothing over his ears, absentmindedly tracing the scar on his right ear.

"Well . . . *almost* the only time. But it's like . . . if I could just show them . . . just get them to see how useful I could be—"

Both Emily and Nugget were unprepared for Ms. Trần's next words:

"I hope you don't think your usefulness is what gives you value."

Girl and dog stared up at Ms. Trần, each equally stunned for their own reasons.

"What gives you value," Ms. Trần continued, "is how kind you are, and how you're the only person like you I've ever met, and how happy you make me every day just by being you."

By instinct, Nugget began to wag his tail gently up and down, remembering when his mother had said almost the exact same things to him, and how much better it had made him feel. Surely Emily would also hear these words and—

"But I'm *not* kind!" Emily cried, and Nugget stopped wagging as Emily stopped petting.

"You're kind to me." Ms. Trần nodded at Nugget. "You're kind to him."

"No, I'm *not*!" Now, when Emily yelled, it was hard to tell if she was yelling at her mother or at herself. "I haven't even named him! That's how not kind I am!"

"He seems to disagree," Ms. Trần observed, and indeed, Nugget had chosen this moment to snuggle back up against Emily's hand, hoping she would get the message: *I'm here for you. Also, please go back to getting that spot behind my ears.*

Ms. Trần followed Nugget's lead, leaning in to plant a kiss on Emily's forehead, before moving back out of the room.

"I'll give you space tonight," she said. "But I want to talk more about this tomorrow, and I won't take no for an answer. You're right—I should start being more honest. But you should too. I've never seen you happier than when you're with that dog. If it's hard for you to open up to me . . . try opening up to him first."

She left, closing the door behind her.

Emily stared after her for a moment, and then, as if she didn't know she was doing it, she resumed stroking Nugget's fur. It was like something her hands just did, keeping themselves occupied while she spoke, the way they'd normally occupy themselves with a hockey stick or a paring knife or a leash.

So Nugget lay there and let himself be petted and gave Emily the space to go on speaking.

Which she did.

"She's not wrong," she said. "But neither am I."

Nugget cocked his head to the side.

"I mean, isn't it crazy that I lashed out at you for being, I don't know, 'ugly'?" Emily continued. "But that's what was really ugly: the way I acted toward you, that first day and all those days after. On some level, I think I was afraid—afraid that you would just be one more thing in my life that would make me feel different, not normal, not *liked*. Meanwhile all you've ever done is want to hang out with me and . . . and almost *help* me, it feels like. You just make me feel . . . accepted. How are you so good at that?"

Well, I spent a lot of time practicing with a porcupine, Nugget wanted to say, but it didn't feel like the right time.

"I mean, I still want those girls to like me. Or at least to just . . . admit that I belong on the team with them. I want it so bad, I can taste it. I don't know why, but I do."

I know why, Nugget thought. *It feels good to be chosen back.*

"But maybe being honest is better than being normal. Because they haven't been there for me. You have. And I need to start being there for you more as well."

Emily gave one last look at the doorway.

"And *that's* me being honest," she said.

She flicked off the light and rolled back onto the bed, settling in for the night.

"I'll give you a name soon. I promise."

Nugget cuddled up into her side.

"I'm just making sure I think of . . . the right . . ."

But Emily must have been tired from her emotional day because she fell asleep so fast that she never got the chance to finish her sentence.

She would never get a chance to think of a name either.

Sorry.

Again.

35
Acceptance

Let's just cut straight to the rough stuff this time, shall we?

This was the day Nugget started to think of himself as Ugly.

It was Emily's next practice. She had marched up the hill to Ronan Park like she was marching into battle, and Nugget had been right there beside her every step of the way. To be honest, he was kind of surprised she hadn't just left him at home after the events of the last practice, but she had squared up her shoulders, looked him in the eyes, and said, "We're not letting them win. You deserve to enjoy that park just as much as they do. More, personally. Let's go."

Now, as they approached the park, Emily held her chin up high, bracing herself for any amount of backlash for daring to stand up to Lexington and Madison. And sure enough, there the co-captains were, waiting for Emily at the edge of the field, each of them . . .

Smiling and waving hello?

More than any insult or attack, this warm greeting threw Emily off her groove. She looked nervously around the park, trying to find Coach Farineau, but of course she was nowhere to be seen; Emily's purposeful stride had caused her to arrive early, and the place was almost empty. It was just her, the captains, and a few girls setting up cones at the far end of the field.

"We're sorry, Emily," said Lexington.

"Yeah." Madison nodded solemnly, her hands clasped behind her back. "We've been pushing you pretty hard. That must have been tough for you. But you have to be tough to keep up with this team, and we had our doubts that you could cut it."

"So we were really doing it *for* you," Lexington explained. "But we're sorry if it didn't *feel* that way. But anyway, it doesn't matter, because after the way you stood up for yourself last time . . . now we see that you're definitely field hockey material. And we're totally committed to making sure everyone knows it."

"O . . . kay," Emily said. "Thank . . . you?"

Nugget didn't believe a single word of what these girls were saying, and from the way he could hear Emily's heart pounding, it seemed they were on the same page.

But then his nose twitched in the air, and to his dismay, he realized that he and Emily weren't on the same page at all. They weren't even reading the same book. Because for once, the smell Emily was radiating in the presence of these two girls wasn't one of fear. It was hope. Hope that this time, maybe, *possibly*, her dreams were coming true. That she was finally about to find acceptance.

So Nugget tried to swallow his doubt. After all, he wanted Emily's dreams to come true too. Right?

Then Madison removed her hands from behind her back.

"We just need you to do one thing," she said, offering something up to Emily.

It was a dog collar.

It was tight and black and spiked on all sides, except in the very front where it said, in big bright letters: UGLY.

"The Gorgons need a mascot," Lexington said. "And Ugly would be *perfect*."

Nugget and Emily both stared at the collar. Now Nugget's heart was pounding just as hard as Emily's. This time, though, they *had* to be on the same page.

At least, Nugget really hoped they were.

"I thought you were done being mean," Emily said. The words came out terribly soft, but each one seemed to exhaust her as if she were shouting at the top of her lungs.

"I mean, if you think about it, it's not mean," Madison said. "That's, like, what a gorgon is, right? Someone ugly enough to turn their enemies into stone? That's *cool*. We *want* Ugly to scare people."

"Don't call him—" Emily stopped herself, took a breath, started again. "I just know people who wouldn't have . . . I mean, most people probably wouldn't like it if you called them Ugly."

"Ugly's not people," Lexington said. "He's a *dog*. He doesn't *care*."

But Nugget did care. He cared a lot. He longed for Emily to look down at him, to see how he was imploring her not to do it. But her eyes were frozen on the gleaming spikes of the collar. And Nugget understood why. That collar represented what Emily longed for: a chance for things to just be easy. To just fit in.

"It doesn't seem like you're really being a team player," Madison said after Emily had paused too long for her liking.

She pulled the collar back toward herself.

Even though he felt bad for Emily, Nugget shuddered with relief: *thank goodness*.

And then, as if being pulled by a sideways gravity, Emily took a step forward, toward the collar.

What?!

"That's not—I'm a *great* player," she protested. "I'm one of the best players on the whole team."

"There's a difference between being a player on a team," Lexington said, "and being a team player."

"Yeah," Madison said. "We want to tell everyone how cool you are and how much we should all have your back. But we need to know *you* have *our* back first. We went to all this trouble of making this collar so your dog could feel included, and now you won't even include him? This shouldn't be a hard choice, Emily. Isn't this what you want?"

Finally, Emily looked down. Normally Nugget was the one silently trying to communicate with humans, but now it was her eyes that silently pleaded: *Help me out here. What do I do?*

Nugget knew what he *wanted* Emily to do. He wanted her to reject them entirely, to walk away, to leave Ronan Park and never come back, or better yet—to tell an adult what Lexington and Madison had been doing all this time so that *they* had to leave and never come back.

But he also knew what he wanted for Emily. He wanted her to feel happy and loved and understood. When she was playing field hockey, she *was* understood. Her talent, her skill, her drive—they were all observed, respected, rewarded. She belonged on that field.

But belonging on that field and belonging on this team were two separate matters entirely.

Nugget wanted to be able to say: *Do it. I understand. It's okay.*

But it wasn't true. Understanding something wasn't the same as it being okay. Hadn't Emily talked about not needing to be normal? Couldn't she see how the ugliest things here were the two souls standing in front of her, asking her to turn on her friend? What good was being accepted by them if their acceptance came at this cost? What good was all the time Nugget had spent with Emily, trying to help her out, to make her feel better—if all it amounted to was this?

In that moment, Nugget decided: If Emily did this, gave

in to these girls, turned on Nugget this way . . . she would be no better than them.

And if Nugget kept begging to be accepted by someone who would treat him this way, then he would be no better than any of them.

Nugget took a single step backward.

Emily noticed this instantly. How couldn't she? Not only were they connected by a leash, but also it was, ever since the day he had come to Trần Phở, the first time Nugget had ever tried to move *away* from Emily Trần rather than closer to her.

And tragically, that was exactly the thing that spurred her into action. Emily seemed to panic, seeing her chance at acceptance slipping through her fingers. It was as if Nugget were a runaway field hockey ball or a rogue onion fallen from the counter. Before he could get any farther—or maybe just before she could stop herself—Emily grabbed the collar from Madison's hands, knelt down, and clasped it around Nugget's neck, all with that same terrible swiftness that made her such a good team player.

For a moment, dog and girl stood there, locked in the same staring contest they'd been in just a few weeks ago, looking into each other's eyes. But that moment had been one of deep understanding between Nugget and Emily.

This moment was different.

Because in this moment there was no more Nugget.

In this moment, he was reminded of all the terrible

disappointments he'd suffered, the losses, the rejections. And he decided that the common factor in all of them was . . . himself.

This was the moment he truly started to think of himself as Ugly.

And somehow Emily must have seen this—a light going out in those brown eyes, a curling downward of the tail, a sinking into the collar—because it was also the exact moment she snapped out of whatever horrible spell she'd been under and came back to reality.

"No," she breathed. Louder, she insisted: *"No."*

She reached out to rip the collar right back off, but her hands were shaking, and Ugly—that was his name now; inside and out, he was Ugly—didn't want her to come near him. He didn't want to let anyone near him ever again. He pulled back. And because Emily had had to remove his leash to put the new collar on, he quickly moved out of her grasp.

"Wait," Emily said, falling forward onto her knees as she tried to get him back. "No— Don't—"

"Good job, Trần," Lexington said from above her. "I wasn't sure you had it in you. I think it looks natural on him, right?"

Which she really shouldn't have said, because now she got to learn what her co-captain had learned just one short practice ago—what it felt like when Emily Trần came flying off the ground at you in full force.

Of course, Emily shouldn't have done that either. Once upon a time, she had been fast enough to catch up with a runaway dog in Ronan Park. Now, overcome with anger and shame, she allowed herself to become distracted. And that distraction gave Ugly a huge head start, allowing him to race away unnoticed. Then by the time anyone did notice, it was too late. He was across the field and tearing down another tier of Ronan Park and another and another, until he disappeared, lost in the glare of the sun bouncing off the faraway bay.

It helped that by now he was an expert at running away. But this time was different from all the times before. This time, it wasn't an act of refusal. It was a decision to embrace who he truly felt he was meant to be: Alone. Unloved. Ugly.

This was an act of acceptance.

Part Three

NUGLY

36

Hunger

Night fell on a cold beach. Black waves crashed on the shore. Out in the lonely distance, the lights of barges parked at the edge of the continental shelf twinkled in and out, fighting and often failing to pierce the distant dark.

And in the scrubby undergrowth of the dunes, a dog hid from the world, shivering all over with something much worse than the evening chill. Once all the light faded from the western sky, there was a chance the dog would haul himself out into the open sight lines of the world—but only a chance. The dog had learned to keep out of sight of humans as much as physically possible. He'd had a lot of chances to learn.

Ugly had been Ugly for two weeks now.

In a lot of ways, he felt he had been Ugly for much longer.

Right now, though, he mostly just felt *hungry*.

Over the past two weeks, he had darted through alleys and dark shadows, emerging only at nightfall, picking scraps out of dumpsters where he could, and moving reluctantly onward where he couldn't, which was all too often. Gradually he'd worked his way north and east until he'd arrived here, at the end of the world. Or at least at the end of dry land.

He'd had days to formulate a plan while hiding here on this sandy beach, but Ugly truly could not think of what he was supposed to do next. Of course, it was hard to think clearly when he was slowly starving, and for some reason it was getting harder and harder for Ugly to run long distances without his breath starting to hiccup. But even if he'd been well-fed, he suspected he'd run out of places to go. He was even more thoroughly lost than the last time he'd left home, and just like last time he wasn't sure he could have found his way back to Emily or Ms. Trần if he wanted to.

And he almost did. Want to. He'd spent a lot of time thinking about what Emily had done, and at this point he didn't even blame her. Not really. Because now he knew the problem was him.

After all, if he was worthy of love, surely he would have found some love he could hold on to by now. So it stood to reason that other people weren't the problem. He was.

He was just too . . . Ugly.

So he didn't show himself to anyone. Not to the joggers who ran across the sand in the morning and not to the fishermen who stood patiently by the jetties in the afternoon. He didn't even show himself to the family who descended on the beach every night in a warm tornado of blankets and bonfires. They had friendly faces and voices and, more to the point, they had food—s'mores, hot dogs, burgers, chips, carrots all laid out every evening and then thrown back into baskets sometime after nightfall. Every night, Ugly watched this spectacle from the high grass until the sand under him was darkened with drool.

But every night, he remembered who he was and how he looked.

And so every night he buried himself deeper in the sand, hoping the roar of the ocean would be louder than the roar of his stomach.

In his hungriest moments, staring at what he had come to think of as the Night Family, Ugly felt his hunger grow into a longing for something more than food. The Night Family's numbers changed every evening—sometimes a man, a woman, and four children; sometimes just the woman, but with two teens and three kids; sometimes six or seven kids, all of varying ages, splashing in and out of the surf and shrieking happily. The family's beach trips seemed to be catch-as-catch-can, conducted with whomever was on hand, and in the chaos and tumult of the siblings bouncing off one another, Ugly saw a reflection of the brothers and sisters he had loved so much in his first-ever home. The way they careened off one another, finding the joke in everything—in splashing too much, or not splashing enough; in throwing their fries to a hungry seagull; in the way one boy, quiet and unshrieking, kept his shirt on to swim, claiming it made him warmer even in the frigid water of the ocean—it all reminded Ugly of Wendy and Bacon and Pepper and Biscuit and Frosty and Cheese Fries and Sprite.

What would they have said if they could see him now? Would they still recognize him as one of their own? As someone who belonged?

No. Ugly didn't belong anywhere. Thinking of the horror in their faces if they saw *his* face, Ugly's resolve to stay hidden grew stronger and stronger.

But every night, Ugly was getting hungrier and hungrier.

He wondered sometimes what would get him first: the hunger or the loneliness.

Jeez.

This is getting pretty dark.

Let's check in with someone happier, shall we?

37

The Happy Seagull

Once upon a time in Boston, there was a very happy seagull. The seagull was happy because every day, it got to wake up and do the number one main thing seagulls love to do: scream at people and steal their food.

Technically this was two main things, but the seagull wasn't terribly bright. This was another big part of why it was so happy.

The seagull flew all over the city, snatching stray meatballs from the streets of the North End and pilfering pupusas from the Salvadoran joints by the piers of East Boston. But every evening, it returned to what it considered its home base: L Street Beach, the long strip of sand and scrub running along the southernmost shore of Southie, which is short for South Boston, which is a weird name in that it is actually north of much of the city, including all of Dorchester.

(It is also, for the record, more or less directly south of East Boston, which is somehow north of the North End. The Boston city planning department strikes again.)

Of course, the seagull didn't know any of this. It just knew that every evening, the L Street Beach transformed into the buffet of a bird's dreams as a loud and happy family arrived and promptly began spilling crumbs of food across the sand, sometimes even throwing fries *directly to* the seagull! This, as far as the seagull was concerned, was a miracle and confirmation that the seagull had done something wonderful in a past life, like being a slightly cooler seagull.

But all was not well in seagull world. Recently a dog had started sneaking around the beach. So far he had gone unnoticed by everyone at eye level, but he was easy to spot if you were a seabird flying overhead. The dog looked like trouble, and not just because of its arresting face and spiked collar. It looked like trouble because it looked *hungry*, and night after night it had begun creeping farther and farther toward the edge of the beach scrub, eyeing the same thing the seagull was eyeing: the bonfire and the happy family around it.

The seagull did not approve of this. At all. That family was its meal ticket. More mouths, more problems, that's how the seagull felt, and it didn't matter how down on your luck you looked. And wow, that dog's luck looked positively *subterranean*.

One night about a week after the arrival of the dog, things came to a head. The seagull was slowly sidling up to the youngest member of the family, who was just absolutely *vaporizing* a chocolate chip cookie, when suddenly it noticed movement out of the corner of its eye.

The dog's desire to eat must have finally won out over its desire to hide because it had emerged from the scrub and begun to totter toward the fire. It crept closer and closer, but hunger had made it weak, and its walk was shaky and slow. The humans hadn't even noticed anyone was approaching.

The seagull had to do something to protect its food source. It was now or never. So it opened its mouth and did the thing it had been doing all its life: It screamed.

"Squawk! Squawk! Squaaaawk!"

At first, this had the desired effect. The humans around the bonfire looked up, startled by the sudden outburst.

But then, something happened that had *never* happened in the seagull's life: One of the humans screamed back.

It was the little one with the cookie, a girl, and she was screeching at the top of her lungs. But she wasn't actually screaming at the seagull. She was pointing in terror and screaming at the dog, and as she did so the other humans jumped up around it to see what was the matter, which blocked the seagull's view of their food *entirely*.

Well, this just hadn't worked out at *all*.

Oh well. With a huffy flap of its wings that functioned as the seagull version of rolling one's eyes, the bird took off from the beach. If it hurried, it could probably beat the dessert rush and snatch a cannoli right out of some poor tourist's hands.

All in all, it was another exciting day in the life of the very happy seagull.

38

Meanwhile, Back at the Beach

The girl who was screaming was named Annie McLaughlin.

You could tell from the way her mother yelled, "Annie McLaughlin, you stop screaming this *instant*!"

"But it's a *monster*!" Annie wailed, pointing at Ugly, who was frozen in fear in the middle of the beach. He knew he shouldn't have come out here. He *knew* it. But he also knew if he didn't eat something soon, nothing else would matter very much at all.

"Oh, honey," Mrs. McLaughlin tutted. "It's not a monster. He's just a stray dog who's—"

Just then, an ocean breeze caused the bonfire to roar up, and Ugly's face was better illuminated for Mrs. McLaughlin to see.

"*Oh,*" she said, and it wasn't the tone of voice Ugly expected at all. "Did . . . did somebody *hurt* that dog?"

"Ooh, what if he's *feral*?" This came from a teenage McLaughlin, his hands up in claws, his grin indicating that the idea of Ugly's ferocity was not so much scary as it was extremely cool and exciting.

"Shut up, Tommy."

"*You* shut up, Bryan!"

"He's not feral," said a third boy softly—the quiet one who always swam in his T-shirt. "Look. He's wearing a collar. He's just a scared, hungry dog."

"Oh." Tommy deflated and kicked at a beach rock. "That's fine too, I guess. Whatever."

"Sam, look for a tag on the collar," Mrs. McLaughlin said. "Someone must be looking for this dog."

The quiet boy—Sam—grabbed a burger from a paper plate and held it out toward Ugly.

"C'mere, boy," Sam said gently. "Come closer. It's okay."

Almost every instinct in Ugly's body screamed to move away, to run out of sight of this child.

Almost every instinct save one. And that was the most important instinct of all.

He crept closer to the boy and the burger.

"There's no tags," Sam said as the dog moved further into the firelight. "No address or anything. It just says . . ."

"What?"

Sam turned to his mother.

"It just says Ugly."

This time, when Mrs. McLaughlin looked at the stray dog, she examined it with a mother's eyes. She frowned, but it was clear the person she was frowning at wasn't the poor animal in front of her.

"On second thought," she said, "maybe we don't need to be in such a rush to find whoever made a collar like that."

Upon being scrutinized so closely—and being reminded of the girls who had made this collar for him—Ugly began to back away.

But then Sam said something that stopped him in his tracks.

"This dog is *not* a monster," he said, with a heated passion that belied his soft voice. "And he is *not* ugly. That shouldn't be his name. We should call him—"

"Who said we were calling him anything?"

"Shut up, Tommy."

"Shut *up*, Bryan!"

"We should call him . . ." Sam barely seemed to hear his brothers. "Not-Ugly. No. N . . . ug . . . ly. Nugly!"

He threw his arms into the air—*eureka!*—and the burger he'd been holding went flying right out of its bun.

With surprising speed for his emaciated frame, the dog leaped, snatched the patty out of the air, and swallowed the thing whole before he had even touched back down on the ground.

"Good boy, Nugly!" Sam said.

Two ears perked up.

A tail started, slowly, to wag.

He was still hungry. He was still determined not to make

the same mistake he'd made so many times before of getting attached and letting himself get hurt.

But for the first time in weeks, the dog standing on the beach remembered his name was *not* Ugly. Once, when he was loved, it had been Nugget. And now, somehow, this boy had stumbled on a name that reminded him of who he'd once been, glided right over how he felt now, and looked forward to some possibly brighter future: *Nugly.*

No longer Nugget, but not just Ugly, the dog who had just been deemed Nugly moved forward and tentatively licked Sam's sandy ankle.

It was a lick that said thank you.

It also said: *Got any more of those burgers?*

And it was what convinced Mrs. McLaughlin, watching from the edge of the blanket, to make an executive decision.

"That dog," she said, "is coming home with us. Now."

39
Triple-Decker; Sandwich

Home, for the McLaughlins, was "the triple-decker," a skinny three-floor apartment building on Old Harbor Street on the south side of Southie. And the McLaughlins were grateful for all three floors of space. On the triple-decker's quietest mornings, there were at minimum ten people banging in and out of the bathrooms, frantically getting ready for the day ahead: Mr. McLaughlin, Mrs. McLaughlin, Mrs. McLaughlin's mother, and the seven McLaughlin children, who were, in order from eldest to youngest: Tommy, Bryan, Nell, Sam, the twins Janey and Joey, and, of course, little Annie McLaughlin.

But that was just the start of it. Because it turned out Nugly was not the only soul who had been taken in at the McLaughlin house. Between cousins in need of a couch to crash on, down-and-out uncles, up-and-up aunts, and various kids' girlfriends, boyfriends, or friend-friends, the triple-decker was permanently stuffed to the gills with people—but also with love, which Mrs. McLaughlin insisted was the secret to making it all work "because it sure as heck isn't the money."

The McLaughlins' resources may have been spread thin,

but they were generous in time, affection, and — this could not be stated enough—food. Within minutes of arriving back at the triple-decker, someone had dug up a dusty old cat bowl from a cupboard, and just when Nugly was filing this away as another good reason not to trust these people, someone else pulled a corned beef sandwich out of the freezer and began heating it up to drop in Nugly's new bowl, causing him to begrudgingly acknowledge that he may in fact be open to the use of said bowl.

While Nugly inhaled his dinner, the McLaughlin children fell about fighting over who got the honor of hosting their new housemate in their room for the night, until Mr. McLaughlin stepped in to clarify that *no one* would be sleeping with the *unknown stray dog* in their room, and by the way, was Mrs. McLaughlin willing to step into the living room and maybe discuss a little bit of her thought process here?

But before anyone could respond to that—and seven or eight people appeared very much to want to respond to that— Sam McLaughlin slipped into his room and reappeared moments later with a wad of bedding, which he dropped in the hall at Nugly's paws.

"If he's going to sleep in the hall," he said, "he should at least be comfy."

Mrs. McLaughlin smiled at her son and then at her husband.

"Great thinking, kiddo," she said.

Nugly was inclined to agree. After weeks of unending wariness and no consistent sleep schedule, he was exhausted. Now suddenly, here he was in a warm home with a full stomach, and he could already feel himself plunging into dreamland. The bedding had no sooner touched the ground than he was curling up in it, tucking his tail under his strawberry nose, allowing himself to let down his guard just a little bit.

Not *all* the way of course. Sleeping in the hallway was just fine by Nugly, who didn't intend to get attached to any of these people. That road only led to heartache.

But as the smell of Sam permeated Nugly's senses—had the boy pulled his own bedding off his own bed? How generous was this kid? No, no, don't think about that—Nugly had to admit that, even if he didn't want to get too cozy with the *people*, he was enjoying getting cozy . . . with . . . their bedding . . .

And just like that, Nugly had fallen into his first sleep in another new home.

40
A Bit of an Odd Chapter

This was a bit of an odd chapter in Nugly's life.

And this was a dog who had been through some pretty odd chapters. He'd lived in a zoo, trying to get close to a porcupine with a chip on its spiky shoulder. He'd lived above a restaurant, trying to get close to a girl who kept her heart closed up and full of secrets.

But now, Nugly was the one trying to stay distant, to stay spiky, to not let anyone in. And he found himself facing not one, not two, but at *minimum* eight or nine people all trying to get close to *him*.

The trouble began the very next morning, when Annie McLaughlin approached Nugly, rubbing the sleep out of her eyes, to apologize for calling him a monster. As a gesture of goodwill she had brought a ratty, well-loved stuffed sheep, and she dropped it on the bedding next to Nugly's face.

"I chew this sometimes," she whispered into his unscarred ear. "I thought you might like to too."

Clearly Nugly was in for a battle here. But he just reminded himself: The more you allowed yourself to rise to the bait of love, the harder it hurt when you inevitably fell again. Once, he had believed family were people you chose who chose you back. But how could he believe that now when family after family had been torn away from him or, worse still, had let him go? His mother and siblings; Taylor and the Vandycks; Lucky and the animals of the Franklin Park Zoo; and the Tràns . . . every time he felt at home somewhere, he lost it.

So he did his best to make sure he never felt at home. Whenever possible, he focused on the negative. For example, there was Mr. McLaughlin's continued, vocal concern that they had brought a strange dog into their home who though polite may have had rabies or worse. Or there was Nell's boyfriend, who visited one day and proclaimed that Nugly's face was "wicked hideous." And always, always, there were the cousins and uncles and other stray visitors who didn't quite understand the McLaughlin children's enthusiasm for their newest boarder, and who eyed Nugly with expressions ranging from pity to disgust.

But the McLaughlins would not be counted out that easily.

For example, upon hearing Mr. McLaughlin insinuate that Nugly may have had rabies, Tommy's excitement about the cool stray dog in his home redoubled even stronger than before, and he started calling his friends to brag about how they didn't have a dog as cool as his.

And when Bryan heard Nell's boyfriend trash-talking Nugly, he yelled that he would pound him if he ever caught him talking like that again, at which point Nell promptly pounded Bryan and then returned to her boyfriend and informed him in no uncertain terms that if he ever *did* talk about Nugly like that again, she would dump him so fast he would set a land speed record for being single.

And every time an unfriendly cousin passed by in the hallway, somehow Sam would magically always be at Nugly's side—appearing silently enough to visibly surprise the cousin in question, which made sense, but also silently enough to surprise Nugly, which was *really* impressive given the usual canine-human detection flowchart and how it tended to go in the opposite direction. But there Sam would be, staring down McLaughlins and McLaughlin-adjacents with a silent look that positively dared them to say something about the dog Sam himself had named.

And the really impressive thing was . . . they very rarely *did* say anything, or at least not anything more than "Ah, sorry, let me just . . . sneak by ya there . . ." before proceeding sheepishly to do just that, leaving Sam to pet that magic spot just behind Nugly's ears in peace.

In the face of all that, you could see how it would be hard for Nugly to stay distant.

Then there was, of course, the other underlying problem, which was that it simply wasn't in any dog's nature to stay distant from its humans, and it certainly wasn't in Nugly's. Some days when Janey and Joey would fight over who could bring him the best stick to play with or who got to walk him to the beach that night, Nugly had to physically restrain himself from running over and drowning them in slobbery kisses. Sometimes his body even started trotting toward them before his brain knew what he was doing.

But then he would remember he was being cool and aloof, and he would go to the other side of the room and sit in the corner, staring at the wall, trying to look like someone who wasn't falling for this whole loving-family act for one second.

But even there, his body simply could not get on board with department policy, letting his tail wag back and forth behind him for all the world to see.

Frankly, it was getting harder and harder to fool anyone.

Then one day, he stopped having to try.

41
The Shirt off His Back

That day had not gotten off to an auspicious start.

Mr. McLaughlin, who had gradually been forced to acknowledge Nugly's persistent habit of neglecting to bite and/or en-flea any of the children, had announced at the breakfast table that he was willing to let Nugly stay with them—on one condition.

"Somebody," he declared to the kitchen at large, as Joey and Bryan threw English muffin chunks at each other, "has to give that darn dog a bath."

Upon hearing this, Nugly, who had been acting as a free-lance muffin chunk disposal service, surreptitiously began to head for the kitchen exit. But somehow—how did he always do this?—Sam McLaughlin appeared where Nugly least expected him, filling up the doorway and bending down to pick Nugly up off the ground, firmly but not ungently, even as the dog wriggled and whined and stuck each of his legs out as straight as he could get them, trying to make himself as much of a pain to carry as possible. With no incentive to make these people like him, Nugly was finally free to do what not *all* but *most* puppies are born wanting to do: rage, *rage,* against the washing of the dog.

Sam just ignored this, stoically taking Nugly up the stairs to the second-floor bathroom, where he dropped Nugly in the tub and started to run the tap.

See? Nugly thought miserably as his splashy attempts to scrabble out of the tub were thwarted by a smooth porcelain surface and a steadfast Sam. *This is why I have trust issues. Well, mostly it's all the other things that have ever happened to me . . . but also it's this.*

As wrapped up as he was in his own suffering, Nugly only dimly registered something odd: Despite all the splashing and crashing going on in the tub, Sam continued, as always, to wear his T-shirt throughout the whole thing, even after it had gotten completely soaked and hung heavily off his skinny frame.

Come to think of it, in a house where it was not uncommon to see the McLaughlin boys—and occasionally, giggling wildly, Annie McLaughlin—running around in various states of undress, Sam was perhaps the one member of the family Nugly had only ever seen fully clothed.

Huh. Weird. Nugly was just about to tease this thought out when another splash of water over his eyes reminded him of more pressing issues, e.g., the fundamental indignity of all life.

A few hours later by Nugly's estimation (and a few minutes later, according to the clock), Sam finally shut the water off and set about toweling Nugly off.

"Good boy," Sam said quietly. "Good Job. You're doing great." And Nugly did his best not to let those words into his heart though they were as soft and fluffy as the towel now wrapped around his body.

Then, mercifully, the two of them exited the bathroom at last.

And ran immediately into Uncle Frank.

In a triple-decker full of proud loudmouths, Uncle Frank was perhaps the proudest, and certainly the loudest. Nugly had heard him holding forth at the many mealtimes he "just happened to drop by" for, going on about every topic he had thoughts on. And Uncle Frank had thoughts on a *lot*: the way the neighborhood needed to change; the way the neighborhood was changing too much; what the Pats should do that season; what his brother-in-law should do at work; and— perhaps most important—why in the *world* they had let a dog into their house who looked like that overrated, plug-ugly, Boston-abandoning Babe Ruth, but ten times less enjoyable to look at.

Worst of all, Uncle Frank was Sam-proof. For the rest of the extended family, Sam's quiet demeanor acted as a sort of surprise judo attack, throwing them off their game and earning their respectful deference to both his presence and Nugly's, even if they were confused as to why they were giving it.

Uncle Frank, though, was not so easily thrown.

"Sammy boy!" he cried, as Sam emerged from the bathroom.

"Hi, Uncle Frank," Sam said, his voice even softer than usual.

"Hey, why the long face?" Uncle Frank grinned. "At least you've *got* a face!"

He flicked his eyes back and forth between Nugly and Sam: *Eh? Get it? Get it???* When Sam did not react, Uncle Frank decided to get it enough for both of them, wheezing with laughter at his own joke.

"Hey, I'm just kidding," he said, clapping Sam on the shoulder. "Lighten up."

"I don't like it when you make fun of him," Sam said.

"Aw, I'm sorry, buddy," Uncle Frank said, though it reminded Nugly of another two girls he knew whose apologies always sounded insincere.

"But look," the man continued, "even the dog likes it! See? He's smiling! Like this!"

He dropped his jaw wide open and stuck his tongue far out one side of his mouth, in a grotesque imitation of what he thought Nugly looked like.

Again Sam did not react.

"I wish," the boy said lowly, "you wouldn't talk about him like that."

Uncle Frank kept chuckling, but his eyes weren't laughing along with the rest of him anymore.

"And I," he said, "wish you wouldn't take everything so seriously. Not everyone's gonna love the way your dog looks. You need to realize that now. You gotta learn how to take a joke, kid."

Sam considered this.

And then he did something Nugly had never seen him do: He grabbed the bottom of his shirt with both hands, and lifted it up to his chin.

Uncle Frank's eyes widened—and so did Nugly's. There, blazing lividly bright on Sam's chest and back, was a sprawling port wine stain: a big, splotchy purple birthmark that wrapped around Sam's torso like a clinging burn.

"Would you make jokes about this?" Sam asked, and for the first time, a waver appeared in his voice; Nugly could tell it was killing him to show this part of himself to anybody. The boy's knees were practically knocking together. This birthmark must have been a huge point of insecurity for him, but still he held Uncle Frank's gaze and added, "Would you tell everyone they should laugh at me because of this?"

The color drained from Uncle Frank's face. This was impressive, as Uncle Frank had a very red face.

"N-no," he stammered. "Of—of course not. My—your mother would kill me."

"*That's* the reason you wouldn't make fun of me?" Sam asked.

Uncle Frank hung his head, looking down at the ground.

This had the notable effect of causing him to look directly at Nugly.

"No," he said again, quieter this time. "It would also be . . . not okay to do." Then after a pause, he added, "Sorry."

Sam nodded. "Thank you," he said.

For a moment, he looked like he was going to lower his shirt back down, covering his birthmark back up.

But then he pulled the shirt all the way off his body, wadding it up into a ball.

"This is covered in wet dog fur," Sam said. "I'm going to go put it in the laundry. And for the record, I *do* love the way my dog looks. Because he looks like who he is, and I love who he is. C'mon, Nugly."

And with that, Sam walked off down the hall, his port wine stain proudly on display for anyone passing by to see.

Nugly took one last look at Uncle Frank, who was still staring, stunned and sheepish, at his feet. Then the dog turned and trotted briskly to catch up with Sam.

And as he did so, he knew: He had lost. Sam and the McLaughlins had just won. From this moment forward, there was simply no point in Nugly's pretending he did not love these people. Because he did. A lot.

And also from that moment forward, it was worth mentioning: Sam McLaughlin never wore his shirt to swim in the ocean ever again.

42

Castle Island

After the Uncle Frank incident, Sam and Nugly started spending more time together. The triple-decker didn't have much by way of a yard to play in, so Sam started taking Nugly for long walks all around Southie. Together they looped around towering cathedrals and squat new condominiums, past fried food joints and fire stations decorated with community murals. On their longest walks, they made it all the way out to Castle Island, a beautiful spit of land at the tip of the city where there was, as astute Boston scholars may have guessed by now, neither a castle *nor* an island. There was, however, a pretty cool old colonial fort and a picturesque walking trail at the edge of the ocean where airplanes regularly flew just a few hundred feet overhead as they prepared to land at Boston Logan Airport. So that was pretty neat.

One day, Nugly was standing on this exact trail, waiting for Sam to return from ordering a hot dog. (For some reason, the cool old colonial fort sold really good hot dogs. Nugly wasn't sure where exactly hot dogs factored into revolutionary military history, but it was his personal opinion that everywhere on Earth should sell really good hot dogs, so he refused to question it.)

He *was* starting to question why the seagull a few yards down the path was glaring at him as if holding a personal grudge when Sam returned from the hot dog stand, tossing Nugly an extra bun to eat. Nugly snapped up the offering eagerly, his heart swelling with gratitude. Behind him, unnoticed, the seagull took off in disgust.

"Don't tell Mom and Dad, okay?" Sam chuckled, watching Nugly dig into the delicious bun. "Bread is okay for dogs, so this should *technically* be fine, but . . . hold on, actually, *are* you okay? You've barely touched your bun."

To be clear, Nugly had already devoured half of the bun in several seconds. But Sam had a point: By Nugly's usual eating standards, eating only *half* a bun was barely eating at all. Something was slowing Nugly down. And now, as he stopped mid-chew, he felt something odd—a hiccup coming up from the back of his windpipe, almost like the hiccups he'd been having recently when running around the city. This one was different, though, seeming to get lost on the way to Nugly's mouth, as if it had taken the wrong exit from the canine's throat and decided to bounce around his stomach before, finally, zooming back up his esophagus and emerging at last in the form of a—

"Buuuuurp."

Sam's jaw dropped. If puppies could have blushed, Nugly

would have done so furiously. Burping was many things, but it was decidedly *not* cute. He looked up at his new best friend, the person whose opinion meant most to him in the world, waiting in fear to see what he would say.

Sam looked back down at Nugly, his mouth still hanging open.

His throat quivered, as if he was trying to say something himself, but couldn't find the words.

Then he found them: *"Braaaaaaap."*

Sam let loose a killer burp of his own, one that dissolved into wild laughter and a wicked grin Nugly hadn't even known the shiest, most withdrawn McLaughlin child was capable of. Nugly didn't know which sound made him happier—the burp or the laugh. He wagged his tail in double time, polishing off the rest of the hot dog bun, letting himself fire off another burp in the process.

Maybe a big part of having a best friend, Nugly reflected as Sam bent over laughing above him, was that you didn't *have* to be cute around them all the time. You just had to be you. And even though the dog didn't understand why he continued to hiccup as they circled Castle Island, it didn't seem to matter. Sam continued to laugh and Nugly's tail continued to wag the entire way home.

43
The Final Betrayal

Ignore that chapter title for a bit. Just pretend you didn't see it. Thanks.

Days at the triple-decker turned into weeks, and summer was turning into fall. September arrived, and the waters of Boston Harbor, already cool to begin with, gradually got too cold for night swimming. Soon after that, the McLaughlin family bonfires came to a halt entirely.

Because it was time for the school year to start.

Between the McLaughlins' varying elementary, middle, and high school schedules, not to mention sports, clubs, and after-school jobs, kids began tumbling in and out of the house at all hours like it was a train station. Luckily the nature of the triple-decker meant there was always an adult around to let Nugly out during the day. And when the afternoons rolled around, he was always there at the window, waiting to greet each individual McLaughlin child when they returned. None, though, got quite the warm greeting that Sam got; the moment he came into view walking up the steep Southie street, Nugly would bark and bark. For the first time in longer than he could remember, Nugly simply didn't care if anyone looked and saw the odd little dog who was making so much noise, because knowing Sam could be brave for Nugly made Nugly want to be brave for Sam.

Though that was another thing: That odd little dog wasn't so little anymore. One cool September day, as Sam knelt to tie his shoes, Nugly stopped in front of the hallway mirror and did something he'd gotten used to trying not to do: He looked at his own reflection.

Nugly was seven months old now. The ongoing mystery of how big he would get was slowly unraveling itself: He had hit a medium size, slightly taller than the shoe cabinet Sam knelt by now. While his growth had not yet stopped completely, it had notably slowed down in just the past month, which Nugly was happy with; he liked his new size, finding it just right for fitting under tables and on couches.

Furthermore, as he transitioned back out of life on the street, he had begun to fill out until he had a nice, solid build, no longer skin and bones but a dog with a confident, adolescent heft. He liked that as well.

But the most remarkable thing of all came when Nugly looked directly at his own face . . .

And found that he liked that too.

This was an exciting new feeling, and not just in relation to the day his face had changed. Even back when he'd considered himself *cute*, the foundation of his self-esteem had rested shakily atop the fear that losing his cuteness would mean losing his value. Now, though, he knew: Cute or ugly, it didn't matter. He looked like who he was, and he was someone lovable with worth who made the people he loved best in life feel better.

Nugly looked in the mirror, and, for possibly the first time in his life, he felt truly at peace.

Okay, now you can remember the chapter title.

It was time for the final betrayal.

Just as Sam and Nugly were ready to bound out onto the street together, Mrs. McLaughlin came up the front steps, letting Sam hold the door open for her while she hoisted her groceries in both arms.

"Oh, wow!" she said, seeing Sam had his shoes on. "You guys are already good to go? I guess Dad told you, huh?"

It was a sign of how in sync Sam and Nugly were at this point that they tilted their heads confusedly to the side in the exact same way.

"What?" Sam asked. "Are we supposed to be going somewhere? I was just going to take Nugly to run around Thomas Park."

That was another thing. Once, going to the park had been an exercise in anxiety for Nugly. But with his new attitude—and with Sam by his side—the park didn't seem so scary.

"Oh. I guess he didn't tell you." Mrs. McLaughlin handed a brown paper bag to Sam, and he dutifully accompanied her to the kitchen to help put the groceries away, leaving the door ajar. Nugly took one more longing look at the beautiful day outside and then followed the two humans.

"Tell me what?" Sam was asking.

"It's not a big deal," Mrs. McLaughlin said, rummaging through the freezer to make space. "Dad and I just made a vet appointment for Nugly."

A vet appointment? Well, that sounded like a big deal to Nugly. Luckily, Sam seemed to agree.

"What kind of vet appointment?"

"Oh, just some minor surgery."

Mrs. McLaughlin turned, smiling, to face her son and his dog.

"We're going to fix Nugly's face," she said.

Nugly's heart dropped through his stomach.

It was the betrayal he had never seen coming.

How could he have? If you had told Nugly at any point in the past that there was a way to fix his face, he would have leaped to take it. Literally—he would have sprung from the ground into your arms, yapping and licking you until you took him immediately to whoever was going to undo what had been done, bringing back the only face he thought anyone could ever love.

But these days, Nugly knew there was nothing wrong with him. He knew his face was lovable, because he knew what it felt like to be unconditionally loved.

Or so he had thought. But now it turned out the McLaughlins were just like everyone else. He'd thought they'd accepted him just as he was, but all this time, they'd only "accepted" him with the intention of changing him, of making sure he didn't make them uncomfortable, the way he'd made Emily Trần uncomfortable or all those kids at Father Patrick's Last Chance Animal Shelter uncomfortable.

Nugly must have whimpered without realizing it, because at that moment, Sam and Mrs. McLaughlin each turned sharply to look down at him.

"Hey, is he okay?" Mrs. McLaughlin asked, her forehead furrowing in concern.

No, Nugly thought, backing away instinctively. *Tell her, Sam. Tell her.*

"It's fine, buddy," Sam said, responding to Nugly rather than his mother. "It's going to be fine."

No. Not Sam too. Nugly just couldn't take it.

So he didn't just take it. He bolted, out of the kitchen, around the corner, and into the front hall, where he startled Tommy, who had apparently just returned from his candlepin bowling club, based on the way he dropped his bowling shoes in surprise.

Through Tommy's legs, Nugly had a clear view of the front door, still wide open, still swinging out onto the bright blue autumn day.

Well, why not? Why not one more time?

Before anyone could stop him, Nugly was out the door, away from the triple-decker, down the steep hill of Old Harbor Street, and out of Southie altogether. One more time, he'd run away.

He didn't know it yet, but it would be the last time. There would be no more chances after this.

It was fitting.

There were a lot of things Nugly didn't know.

44
What Nugly Didn't Know

What Nugly didn't know was this: Back in Southie, the entire McLaughlin clan—which meant, honestly, a sizable chunk of Southie—was absolutely frantic.

"Nugly!" called Tommy.

"Have you seen this dog?" Janey asked at one end of the street, as at the other end of the street, Annie was asking, "Have you seen this dog?" Each of them thrust phones into the faces of pedestrians, holding up magnified pictures of Nugly.

"Wait," said Nell's boyfriend, who had been called to the scene to help with the search party. "Since when does Annie have a phone?"

"Oh," Nell said offhandedly, "I gave her yours. Now, come on! Keep up!"

As the older McLaughlin kids fanned out across the long streets of South Boston, Sam and his parents were headed in Nugly's last known direction, south and west. Together, Mr. and Mrs. McLaughlin formed a sort of frenzied communications hub. Mr. McLaughlin had called the police first, was calling animal control now, and while he'd never have admitted it, if animal control didn't pan out, he was going to call City Hall next. Mrs. McLaughlin, meanwhile, was on the phone with the veterinarian's office.

"I'm so sorry, Dr. Sheynberg," she was saying. "We've completely lost him. What should we do?"

As they hurried past Moakley Park, they passed Bryan, who was trying, in his own way, to help, mainly by badgering a bewildered Little League coach.

"You *must* have seen him. He's got—his face is really—well, his tongue hangs out like . . . *thith*. And—oh! He'th got thith brown thtripe running acrothth hith nothe!"

"Pardon me," Dr. Sheynberg said, crackling on the other end of Mrs. McLaughlin's phone call. "Did your son just mention a brown thtri—a brown stripe?"

"Yes, he did." Mrs. McLaughlin waved Bryan over. "Why? Is that important?"

"Just curious," Dr. Sheynberg said. "Probably nothing. That's just . . . the second time this year I've heard from a family about a dog with a brown stripe running away. I remember because they were some of my best clients, and it was right before they moved away to San Fran—"

"Yeah, okay, Doc, whatever," said Bryan. "She asked for help, not your life story." And with that, he darted across the grass to stop someone else. "Hey! Hey, buddy!"

"You'll have to excuse him," Mrs. McLaughlin sighed into the phone. "We all really love this dog."

"I completely understand," said Dr. Sheynberg. "In fact—drop me your location. I'm coming to look too."

"Oh—you really don't have to—"

But to Mrs. McLaughlin's surprise, Dr. Sheynberg had already hung up.

Normally, she might have questioned why this veterinarian was behaving so oddly, but today, she didn't have time. She just dropped her location on her phone, as asked, and then slipped her phone into her pocket to jog after her children.

Sam, meanwhile, was hundreds of feet ahead of his family, currently so focused on his own phone that he hadn't noticed anything happening behind him. The moment they'd realized Nugly was gone, Sam had begun posting on every online neighborhood group he could think of, alerting anyone and everyone of the lost dog in their area and what he looked like.

Now each new notification sent off simultaneous shock waves of panic and excitement in Sam's stomach. The comments had begun to roll in:

Yeah, I saw a dog like that. Nearly scared the life out of me! Intersection of Dot Ave and Howell.

Think I saw him but he was running too fast for me to get a good look—was headed south and west on Columbia Road.

Sam closed the comment window just long enough to open Google Maps and make sure he was following the path laid out by the comment trail. He was—and with single-minded dedication too. A truck horn honked and Mrs. McLaughlin cried out as Sam hurried across a gigantic roundabout, his eyes glued to his phone, devoted only to the pursuit of his lost dog, who, by the sounds of it, had disappeared into Dorchester ten minutes ago.

But why run that way?

Sam was pretty sure he knew why Nugly *had* run away. He was a little embarrassed about the idea of saying it out loud and yet he was sure of what he had seen in Nugly's eyes. That much he understood.

But why run to *Dorchester*?

Where had Nugly *gone*?

45
Where, Why, and How

You've heard a few times by now that when it came to the city of Boston, your average human would have found it impossible to navigate without help, let alone your average dog. And that was still true.

But Nugly was no longer your average *anything*.

After so much time spent walking, running, and hiding in Boston's streets, Nugly had developed a sense of the city that went deeper than any knowledge of street signs or addresses. It was a knowledge that lived in the bones and the body, an inexpressible ability to sense where you were going by the way the terrain sloped up and down, the way the sun shifted from right to left, the way not just individual storefronts but entire *neighborhoods* smelled differently from one another.

So when Nugly ran back toward where he'd once come from, back in another life, it wasn't really an intentional decision. It was guided purely by subconscious instinct, a yearning to return to what was familiar, to go to the last place he had felt even close to safe.

All of which was how he wound up approaching, half an

hour later, a park so large it could have been a small city itself, one ringed by dense forest and containing a giant stadium, a ruin-strewn hill, and a strange-smelling village of huts and tents.

Before he'd even known he was doing it, Nugly had run right back to Franklin Park.

By the time he was passing the bear cages, though, Nugly *very much* knew what he was doing. He was trying to return to the zoo, to Lucky, to a place where wild animals could seek refuge. But could they? Could *he*? The zoo had already done its best to smoke him out the last time he was there. What was his plan now? He didn't have one. He was flying by the seat of his pants.

So much so, in fact, that he hadn't noticed what lined some of the trees and poles he had just run past: stapled, weather-torn posters, each of which bore a picture of a distinctive-looking face, and each of which said over torn-off phone numbers: HAVE YOU SEEN THIS DOG?

This was one more thing Nugly did not know: The McLaughlins were not the only ones who had been looking for him.

No time for that now. Nugly had places to be—and it was taking him longer than he expected to get there. The last time he had approached the zoo, it had been in the dead of night and he'd been distracted by his new porcupine friend. Now, in the middle of the day, he realized that between the bear cages and the zoo lay a vast, flat playing field.

A field that smelled distinctly of something familiar. Something that reeked of cork and rubber. Rubber with a licorice tang so strong that you almost had to wonder: Did rubber *actually* taste like licorice? Or did all licorice just taste . . . like . . .

Field hockey.

Another thing Nugly had not known: Between the bear cages and the back entrance of the Franklin Park Zoo was the Playstead, one of the Boston Parks and Recreation Department's finest athletic fields, and exactly the kind of place you might come to if you were, say, a small field hockey team who had been practicing in your own neighborhood all summer long in anticipation of September, when competition season began and big matches started popping up all around the city.

And one last, very crucial thing that Nugly didn't know: About twenty yards behind him, a hockey mom who was a prolific poster on the community watch groups of *several* neighborhoods, at least one of which she actually lived in, whipped her phone out to take a photo and reply to some urgent posts she had just seen online right before entering the park.

Nugly was too busy panicking to notice any of these things, frozen in the middle of the field. The scent of hockey equipment reminded him of things he didn't want to remember: Lexington; Madison; the pain of looking into Emily Trần's eyes.

But come on. What were the odds that he was actually going to *run into* any of those girls right now? Practically zero, right?

Well, the odds must have been zero. Because when he turned to start running again and promptly froze in place, it wasn't because he had seen any of those girls.

It was because he had seen Katie and Shanna.

"No way," Shanna breathed, pointing at Nugly with her hockey stick as if she had just seen a ghost. "Is that—"

"It *is*," Katie said. "It's—Emily, are you here? He's here! *The dog is here!*"

Before Nugly could react, the loudest cry he'd ever heard rang out across Franklin Park.

And with that same old incredible speed, Emily Trần was racing toward Nugly, and then *throwing* herself toward him, hurling herself across the grass in the most enthusiastic, flawlessly executed slide tackle ever to turn into a hug.

"You're *back*!" Emily cried—as in, really cried, as in, was very much crying real tears all over Nugly, tears that smelled just as strongly of joy as they did of sorrow. "I'm *sorry*! I'm so sorry. I should never have listened to those girls, not even for a . . . I should have told someone—I *did* tell someone, actually—and it got so much better, but I should have done it sooner, because I just kept looking for you every single day. I never stopped—*Mom!*"

The following sound was a strange combination of

clattering and squishing, as Linh Trần looked over from the parking lot, saw the scene occurring on the Playstead, and dropped an industrial kitchen tray full of orange slices to the ground. Then she was running as well, not nearly as fast as her daughter but with just as much enthusiasm, to throw her arms around Emily and thus around Nugly in turn.

They all lay tangled up there for, well, who knew how long. Nugly certainly couldn't tell. World and time had fallen away; there were only the Trầns, their embrace, and the sounds of relief and joy they were all making.

Until suddenly the world came back.

"Who are you?" came a voice from above.

"And how do you know our dog?"

46

Reunions

Here is a rough list of who was standing around Nugly at this time: Nine or ten McLaughlins. One befuddled boyfriend. Half a team of Gorgons. Emily and Linh Trần. Several curious onlookers who'd just wanted to see what was going on. And, huffing and out of breath, arguably the most in demand veterinarian in the southern Boston area.

Here is what they were all listening to:

". . . but it was too late for me to go catch him," Emily explained. "It should never have happened. I should have reported the bullying earlier, but I'd never wanted to make a fuss. But the moment he ran away . . . none of it mattered. I realized I wanted to make the biggest fuss in the world. I told my coach. I told my mom. The girls got kicked off the team. But it didn't matter. I was just so sad he was gone, and that he thought I'd done that to him."

Some members of the crowd muttered to themselves, but Sam McLaughlin nodded in complete understanding.

"It's a terrible feeling," he said. "I know this sounds weird, but I think Nugly heard us talking about giving him surgery to fix his face, and he got upset, and that's when he ran away."

Dr. Sheynberg chuckled and wiped his glasses. "Are you sure he didn't just get spooked by a loud noise or something like that?" he asked gently. "I know many dogs seem very intelligent, but I'm not sure Nugly can actually *understand* every word you say around him—"

"Yes, he can."

Sam McLaughlin and Emily Trần blurted this at the exact same time. Then they looked at each other with the exact same look of surprise.

Then everyone looked at Nugly.

Who just looked back up and wagged his tail.

"Well—" Dr. Sheynberg began.

"Wait," Emily Trần cut in. "You were going to give him *surgery*?"

"Yes," Sam said, "but it's not what it sounds like. Mom, tell her what you told me."

"Yes, of course." Mrs. McLaughlin nodded and turned to address the crowd. At this point, it required a pretty wide turn. Most of the opposing team and a referee had come over, wondering where half their players had gone.

"Nugly *needs* surgery," Mrs. McLaughlin announced, "*not* for how he looks, but for his *health*. We noticed him breathing heavily when he ran long distances or went up and down our stairs and occasionally he has trouble eating. We called Dr.

Sheynberg, and he realized those were all lingering after-effects due to the injuries he got in the first place. We wanted to take him to the vet to get help for his respiratory and alimentary issues—but his face is going to look exactly the same."

Here, she smiled down at Nugly.

"And we wouldn't have it any other way. We love him just the way he is."

"That's right," Dr. Sheynberg confirmed. "The, uh, surgery part, I mean. The other part, I accept on faith. But it reminds me . . . If I could just . . ."

Dr. Sheynberg's voice trailed off, and about twenty people craned their heads to see what he was doing. Which, it turned out, was getting out his phone to place a call on FaceTime.

"Pardon me," he told the crowd, while the other end of the line began to ring. "I just wanted to check something."

Whoever he was calling picked up.

"Hello?"

Nugly's ears perked up. Where did he know that voice from?

"Yes, hello, Lynn. Sorry to bother you unexpectedly, but this is Dr. Sheynberg. I was wondering—could you put Taylor on the phone?"

No.

It *couldn't* be.

The voice on the other end of the line, who Nugly now *definitely* recognized, said, "Well, I—sure, I don't see why not. *Taylor!* Could you come over here?"

And then, it turned out, it very much *could* be.

Because when Dr. Sheynberg turned his phone screen to face directly down at Nugly, there was Taylor Vandyck, looking confusedly into the camera.

"Taylor," Dr. Sheynberg said, "this is going to be a little confusing, but I remembered how heartbroken you were when your favorite puppy went missing just before you moved away. So I wanted to make absolutely sure of something. This may be hard to make out over the phone, especially since he looks so different, but . . . do you think there's any chance that this may be the dog that you lost?"

The suspenseful hush that fell over the crowd was particularly impressive when you realized that just about none of them knew what in the world was going on or who in the world this dog was.

But no one hung in that suspense more than the dog in question.

He had imagined this moment countless times in the last several months: What would happen if *she*, the first human he had ever fallen in love with, saw him now? Whether or not she would like how he looked was one thing; what really worried him was would she even *recognize* him as himself? After all these months he'd spent finding himself, he wanted to believe there was some true core to him that shone through. But if she didn't feel the same—

He didn't even have time to finish the thought before Taylor squinted at the stripe on his nose, gasped, and cried out:

"Nugget!"

The crowd rippled and murmured, but all Nugly—all *Nugget*—had ears for was the sound of Taylor squealing, turning away from the camera and yelling, "Dad! Dad! Come he—wait! *Wendy! Come here! It's him! It's Nugget!"*

And as if the multifamily reunion hadn't been enough, there she was, appearing on the screen with possibly the most expressive face she had ever made in her life: Nugget's mother.

Two dogs began barking joyously at each other from opposite sides of a continent.

"Mom! Mom! Hi, Mom!"

"Nugget!" The phone shook as Wendy tried to leap up toward the screen.

"You recognized me? You didn't forget about me?" Nugly couldn't stop himself from asking. He knew it was childish, but if you couldn't ask childish questions of your mother, who could you ask?

"I think about you every day," Wendy said urgently. "And I'd recognize you anywhere. You're family."

The barking continued even when Dr. Sheynberg pulled the phone back to his ear to try to communicate what was happening to the ecstatic but baffled Vandyck household.

"No, it's—yes, he seems fine—I mean, he seems to have

had a *very* busy social life, but—I'm sorry, I'm going to have to put your dog on mute—"

"Wow." That was Mrs. McLaughlin, clapping her hands on Sam's shoulders. "Clearly we all have a *lot* to talk about."

"I agree." That was Linh Trần, smiling and extending a hand that Mrs. McLaughlin and Sam were both happy to shake.

"Wait, Emily," said Shanna. "Don't we have, like, a game to get to?"

"Right!" Emily flushed, looking over her shoulder at the small field hockey army she had brought to a standstill. To the McLaughlins, she said, "I'm sorry. I know this is poor timing, but, well, I *am* the new captain, so . . ."

"Oh!" Mrs. McLaughlin smiled. "Congratulations!"

"*Co*-captain," Katie cut in, pointing at the badge on her jersey. "They don't make you the *sole* captain just because they catch you fighting with *both* of the previous co-captains."

Emily laughed nervously, glancing at her mom to make sure she wasn't in trouble, but Ms. Trần just shrugged and smiled.

"I always said you needed to go out and be a real kid . . . and, boy, did you ever." Then she turned to the McLaughlins as well. "She's very good, for the record. Would you like to stay and watch?"

"We'd love to," Mrs. McLaughlin said, and half a dozen kids nodded in enthusiastic agreement.

"Okay. Sure. Great." Mr. McLaughlin clapped his hands together, a little bewildered by everything, but pleased that things seemed to be trending in an upward direction. "But *after* that . . . is there anywhere *else* we could go to sit down and have a nice talk?"

Ms. Tràn's smile only grew wider.

"I happen to know a good restaurant," she said, and Emily grinned as well.

"Great! That's great." Mr. McLaughlin threw his hands up in the air, as if trying to surrender control of a situation he had never actually controlled. "Then play on!"

"And will someone get a leash on that dog," joked Dr. Sheynberg. "Otherwise he might run away *again!*"

"I don't think that'll be necessary." Sam smiled down at his dog. "I think he's done running away. Isn't that right, boy?"

Nugget—Nugly—*not* Ugly—looked up at all his families, gathered here together: the McLaughlins; the Tràns; and, thanks to Dr. Sheynberg, his first and forever family, Wendy and the Vandycks. All of them looked back at him expectantly.

It was a bit overwhelming.

But love had always been overwhelming for Nugly. He'd been born with more love than he knew what to do with, and over the course of his life, that love had lifted him up and torn him apart. What did you do with love like that?

Looking at everyone now, an answer occurred to him:

237

Maybe you went out and chose yourself a *lot* of family and loved them unconditionally and let yourself be loved in return. Even if it was scary.

So Nugly did the scary, overwhelming, exciting number one main thing: He let himself be loved.

"Woof!"

Nugly leaped to his feet, ready to follow all his families wherever they went.

"Huh," Bryan said. "Maybe he *can* understand what we're saying."

"Professionally speaking, I doubt it," said Dr. Sheynberg.

"Read the room, Doc," Bryan said.

With that, all Nugly's families set off toward the Playstead stands, chattering happily among themselves, their favorite dog in tow.

Well, *almost* all his families. Briefly, Nugly stopped to look back at the entrance to the Franklin Park Zoo. Love could do a lot of things, but sadly, it could never lift him back over the gates of—

"Oh, yeah, that's right," Emily said, noticing this right away. "Mom, didn't you say the shelter found him living in the *zoo*? We should totally take him there sometime."

"Whoa, wait. We own a *wild zoo dog*?" Tommy breathed. *"Awesome!"*

Okay, maybe love could do anything.

"Emily!" Katie exclaimed with uncharacteristic fervor.

"I know you have just been reunited with your miracle dog, but we will *forfeit* the *game* if you keep stopping to *appreciate the miracle*!"

"Coming! I'm coming!"

And with *that*, they *really* set off.

For the last time.

Promise.

47

How Nugly Looked

It would be very easy to tell you how Nugly looked. You've read about that exact subject quite a bit already.

It might have been more interesting to tell you how Nugly *appeared*.

For example: As Nugly darted this way and that at the edge of the field, yanking at the leash every time Emily dribbled past at lightning speed, he *looked* like any other unruly dog, desperate to chase after whichever zooming ball had just flown through his line of sight.

But to the informed observer, Nugly *appeared*—to an extent that even Dr. Sheynberg had to admit was uncanny for a dog—to be not simply unruly but *proud*, as if he were cheering Emily on while she led her team to field hockey glory. He was not alone in this either. With the combined forces of the McLaughlins and their hangers-on, the Gorgons' cheering section that day was twice as large and half again as loud and rambunctious as it had ever been before. Bryan and Tommy had managed to download noisemaker apps to their phones; Janey and Joey jumped up and down every time Emily got a shot on goal; and though Sam had his hands full trying to keep Nugly from yanking the leash out of his grasp, he still managed to clap and exclaim under his breath each time one of those shots went in. He had plenty of opportunities to do so. In seemingly no time at all, Emily and her cheering squad led the Gorgons to a decisive victory.

Nugly could not have appeared happier.

Another example: Later, when the Tràns, McLaughlins, and Vandycks (who were calling in via video chat) all sat down together at Tràn Phở's outdoor seating area, Nugly may have *looked* a bit twitchy, his head whipping back and forth from one human to the next, but he *appeared* to be completely besotted with every one of them and every part of the experience— especially once the shrimp rolls came out and Annie began dropping them clandestinely under the table.

"I mean, this really is a *wonderful* establishment," Mrs. McLaughlin enthused. "I can see how he must have loved it here."

"Thank you. And thank *you*." Ms. Tràn smiled as Mr. Adefolalu finished laying out the condiments and pulled up a seat next to them. "But you've clearly taken very good care of him as well. Look how much he's filled out!"

Nugly beamed at the compliment. His sister Pepper would have been so proud.

"Maybe he could stay with both of you," Taylor suggested over the phone. "Like, he could go back and forth."

"Taylor," Mr. Vandyck said, "I don't think that's our place to—"

"That sounds great," Emily and Sam said, in complete agreement once again, and once again stopping to look at each other in surprise.

"What did you say your name was?" Emily asked.

"Sam. You're a great player by the way."

Under the table, Nugly perked up—notable, since his current perkiness level was already remarkably high. Normally when Sam spoke to strangers, he did so quietly and shyly, as if worried about taking up too much space. Heck, he spoke that way to his own family. But just now introducing himself to Emily, Sam had sounded not just confident, he'd sounded . . . comfortable. And Emily smelled much the same way. It was as if the two of them recognized something in each other, a resonant quality that made them feel instantly at ease.

"Thanks. And thanks for looking after . . . Nugly," Emily said, still adjusting to the new name. "I can tell he really likes you."

"Thanks." Sam grinned. "He's clearly crazy about you. Maybe we could walk him together sometime. Have you ever been to Castle Island?"

"Whoa!" Emily's face lit up. "I'd love that! We have a *castle* on an *island*?!"

"We *really need* to get you out of this restaurant more," Ms. Trần sighed.

48
One Final Example

A month later, when Emily and Sam took Nugly back to the Franklin Park Zoo, he may have *looked* a bit out of place, a domesticated pet wandering through a globe-spanning assortment of exotic animals. But he *appeared* completely at home, eagerly pulling at the leash the moment the doors opened for visitors.

"Jeez!" Sam almost fell forward trying to keep up with Nugly. "Guess he *really* wanted to come here!"

"Maybe we should have brought him here earlier," Emily said, grabbing Sam's elbow and pulling him back upright even as they followed Nugly's brisk lead.

"I dunno." Sam smiled warmly. "I think Castle Island was worth it. And I'm really glad you showed me Ronan Park."

Since that day at Trần Phở, they'd been going on joint walks every week. It was a great way to hand Nugly off as he shuttled back and forth between the triple-decker and Trần Phở, but more than that it was becoming a ritual Sam and Emily looked forward to in and of itself.

It wasn't like they hadn't had friends before. It was just

that athletic Emily's friends had mostly all been on her sports team and shy Sam's friends were mostly all, well, his family members.

Oh, and a dog. They'd both become very good friends with a dog.

"Where is he *going*?" Emily laughed, picking up the pace as the dog in question rounded a corner and nearly skidded on a patch of fallen leaves. It was a beautiful October day in Massachusetts, and dustings of red and yellow littered the ground, giving the zoo an even more vibrant air than it usually had.

Wherever Nugly was going, he seemed to be changing his mind sharply as he zigged one way and then zagged another.

In truth, he'd been about to detour by his old friends the red pandas to say hi before remembering they were primarily nocturnal animals and probably all asleep. He felt this would be complicated to explain to Emily and Sam, so he had chosen to keep running toward his original destination, racing past the the gorilla hut, past the sheep pens, and up to the cage of—

"The porcupine exhibit?" Emily asked, hands on her hips, looking completely unbothered by their sprint, while Sam put his hands on his knees and huffed and puffed. "Why would he take us *here*?"

But the answer was already crawling out of its log, ready for another day of entertaining children, the same as the last day and the day before that, in a life in which nothing would ever change or—

"Eish!"

Lucky leaped a foot in the air and released a squeak so loud that Sam and Emily both jumped as well.

Nugly, though, just smiled. You'd think someone reacting to him like he was a frightening apparition might have upset Nugly, but he didn't take it too personally. After all, he'd thought Lucky was a monster the first time they'd met, and look how that had turned out.

And indeed, once he'd touched back down on the ground, Lucky squinted at the face in front of him, wiggled his nose, and said:

"*Kid?!*"

"Hi, Lucky!" Nugly smiled. "What do you think of my new look? I got it for you."

Lucky paused, opened his mouth, closed it, and took a moment to groom his quills, as if he couldn't be bothered to reply too quickly.

And then he said, "You went out and got some character, kid. Good for you."

And with the happy reunion that followed, Emily and Sam were let in on another secret they'd never be able to convince Dr. Sheynberg about if they tried: the fact that their dog and a South African porcupine were best friends.

As Nugly bounded around the fence, happily barking out

the entire saga of what had happened since he last saw Lucky, he *looked* like a lot of things: like a lightning streak of brown and white, dancing around the warm brown and black of Lucky's amused and patiently listening face; like a newborn puppy again, leaping and yipping around Sam's and Emily's ankles; like a dog who had been running all his life, just from the way he moved so fast that he practically blurred.

But he *appeared* to be done with a certain kind of running forever. Because he wasn't running away anymore—he was running *toward*, straight toward all the people and places he had chosen that had, in the end, chosen him back.

Nugly was with his family.

He was finally home.

ACKNOWLEDGMENTS

It took an entire city's worth of people to raise Nugly, and it took just about that many people to raise *Nugly* as well.

First and foremost, thanks are due to my editor, Orlando Dos Reis, who has gotten me over the finish line of four books now, and for whom I am more grateful with each book. His willingness to get on the phone and talk out even the most granular of story beats or sticking points has made me a better writer, collaborator, and communicator, to say nothing of what it's done for this book. In these ways and more, Orlando improves the world by being himself.

Thanks as well to Scholastic's superhumanly thorough production team, including Mary Kate Garmire, Rye White, Priscilla Eakeley, Jessica Rozler, Marinda Valenti, and Cady Zeng, and to Angelo Rinaldi, who not only gave this book a cover I *immediately* sent to all my friends, but who somehow saw Nugly exactly the way I saw him. Linh Vu helped with the words and world of the Trầns; gratitude is due to her as well.

I also had some unofficial helpers who deserve an official thank-you. This book would not exist without Dan Reardon, who not only introduced me to Dorchester but, in playing the world's most gracious tour guide and host, helped me fall in love with it. He's also responsible for the Eastie shout-out, come to think of it, and is just great company to boot. And I cannot thank Brad Latilla-Campbell enough for helping Lucky speak the way he does, or recommend enough speaking to Brad Latilla-Campbell in general.

This book was written between August 2021 and August 2022, and in that year, many people helped just by being around, or listening to me, or helping me move(!). Those people include, but are not limited to: Billy, Nico, Nick, Andrew, Jules, Julianna, Gianina, Jack, Paul, Allie, Dylan, Mike, Maddie, Krista, Jake, Bugra, and Ahmed. Earning their own category are the people who invited me to leave my apartment and come write at their place, or at least someplace other than my apartment, for a while: Micah and Tara, Pat and Sara, Daniel, Danna, Chris, and Scott (and of course Gordy, Olive, Morris, and Fran). And combining these two categories, along with the categories of mentor, friend, and killer event planner, is David Levithan, who was there the day this book started, there the day this book finished, and to whom is owed residuals of any joy felt on those days and in between.

As always, thank you to the Q train, with a special thanks this time to the Staten Island Railway.

Okay, we're nearing the end now. Here are some big ones: Thank you to the staff of the Franklin Park Zoo, and thank you to Pho Le Restaurant in Dorchester; if anything about

Part Two of this book made you hungry, I recommend getting a great meal on Dot Ave whenever you get the chance. Thanks to those whose names are in this book: Taylor, Sam, Thomas, and a few others besides who may or may not find out for themselves.

Thank you to Bryan for becoming my favorite reason to visit my favorite city.

Thank you to my family for being the entire reason I was able to pursue my love of reading, writing, Boston, and/or dogs.

And thank you to Liffey, who really only helped with that last part, but did it *really* well. Now, *that's* a dog with character. We love you very much.

ABOUT THE AUTHOR

M. C. Ross is an author and playwright living in New York City. His other books include *A Dog's Porpoise* and *Game Over*. He has been writing books about dogs since the first grade, when he wrote a book about going to outer space with his Labrador retriever. He still writes books about dogs, but his handwriting is slightly better. For more information, please visit mcrosswrites.com.